SACKED AND SLEIGHED

AURELIA KNIGHT

Copyright © 2023 by Aurelia Knight

All rights reserved.

No part of this book may be reproduced in any form or by any electronic or mechanical means, including information storage and retrieval systems, without written permission from the author, except for the use of brief quotations in a book review.

Any likeness to real people is circumstantial.

CONTENT WARNING

Sacked and Sleighed is a very dark **Christmas** Novella with triggering themes and content throughout. This is a quick, smutty read with a fun connection to Stolen Obsessions, but no major tie-ins! This is a loose Saint Nick retelling, but contains no magic other than the Christmas kind.

This book contains graphic, violent and sexual content that may be upsetting to some readers. The following lists some, not all, of the potentially sensitive subjects included. If you have a specific concern please reach out on www.Aurelia Knight.com or in Aurelia's Facebook group Aurelia's Illicit Library.

> Dub/non-con, murder, historic child abuse, breath play, stalking, abduction, somnophilia, drugging, Stockholm syndrome, and holiday puns.

DEDICATION

This book is dedicated to all the overworked, over-shopped, dark romance lovers who just want to be cuddly underneath the tree while getting vicariously railed by a masked Christmas stalker.

CHAPTER 1
BIANCA

"JINGLE BELLS, JINGLE BELLS," I half-heartedly sing as I shake my bell and pray for a time warp that brings me to the end of my shift. The mall teems with activity around Santa's Village, with people Christmas shopping and chatting in all directions. The warm scent of cinnamon tickles my nose.

"Sample? Sample?" the pretzel girl asks the moms standing in line as she walks by. Several of them accept, and my stomach growls. I didn't have a chance to eat between class and my shift.

"Jingle all the way!" My jet-black braids frame my breasts as I bounce lightly from foot to foot, doing my best to make things Christmasy and fun when I'd rather be anywhere else. I look over and catch Ralph, our resident Santa, staring. I slow the shaking to something that doesn't rock my tits, rolling my eyes at the old man as I turn my back on him.

"Pervert."

"Don't be so sensitive, Bianca," he calls from his oversized red chair.

"Stop it, Ralph," my best friend and co-elf Katie intervenes. She has a soft spot for the old man that I don't share even though I've worked with him for six Christmas seasons.

He's not so bad. He's never said anything too disgusting or touched me. I've heard horror stories from other girls about getting groped regularly by the Santas at their malls in the odd times I covered somewhere else. The holiday bizz isn't all pretty.

I'm only mildly embarrassed by Ralph but humiliated by how red I know my cheeks are. The stiff collar of my elf costume scratches my neck, and the brim of my pointy green hat squeezes my ears. My toes ache from the shape of my pointy elf shoes, and I have two more hours before I can change. This is misery.

"More enthusiasm, Bee," Katie encourages. She's bouncing all over the place, and I'm pretty sure her cluelessness and D cup are why Ralph likes her so much. Her long blond hair and sweet upturned nose give her a perfectly elfin appearance, and she's stunning. She's also a late bloomer and not used to the effect she has on men.

This is her first year working as an elf for Santa's Village. This is year six for me, and I'm about as sick of the job as I am of struggling to make ends meet. I'm almost done with school, though. Just a few more months.

"This is fun, Bee. I don't know why you complain." She rings her bell, not really keeping time with the music playing, and waves at the little girls in line.

"The costume smells like shit, and I'm not allowed to wash it." Something about the felt falling apart.

She scolds me with her bright blue eyes, but I'm far enough away that none of the kids in line hear what I say. Just to prove me wrong, a little girl walking past the booth on the other side laughs and points at me. Her mother covers her ears and leads her faster through the mall, shaking her head and muttering.

"Darn." I know better than to curse in costume. I've been donning my pointy bell shoes and braiding tinsel into my hair for long enough to be a seasoned pro, but this year, I'm tired, and my nerves are shot. I fidget with the garter belt holding up my candy cane thigh-high socks. My gaze darts around the mall, and I forget to ring my bell entirely as the song shifts to the next one.

"Bianca, what is going on with you? You've been acting weird for weeks." Katie nudges me toward the little goody bags. I grab one for the little boy who just finished with Santa and smile as I send him back to his mom.

"I'm worried about my abnormal psych final." It's only half a lie.

"Bee, you've studied so much. There's no way this is—"

At that moment, a little girl steps up in line to meet Santa. I grab her hand to lead her over to Ralph and put her on his lap.

As Katie snaps a few pictures, the little girl asks for everything she wants. I look around the mall. The food court bustles in the distance, and the department store on the other end has a line of people out the door. At least a thousand people are between the different floors, but one particular person's presence needles me. He's close. I can feel it.

I help the girl down and hold her hand as I take her to the little white gate. She smiles up at me with her front teeth missing.

"You're really pretty for an elf, and tall."

"Thanks. You're really pretty too." I grab a goody bag for her as we pass the table and throw in a few extra stickers while Katie talks her mom into the upgraded photo package.

"The man over there said you're the prettiest elf, and he asked me to give you this. He also said your name is Bianca, and that means white in Italian, and that you're his princess, like Snow White." She hands me a small card tucked into an envelope with a familiar flourish.

My heart stops, then picks up in double time. I knew he was here, close enough to watch me. He's so damn patient, so constant, the most dependable thing in my life.

"Thanks, sweetie, but don't talk to strangers. Okay?"

She nods, understanding the point easily. "That's what Mom usually says, but the man was so handsome she was talking to him too." She giggles conspiratorially. "My daddy got mad and said, 'What are you doing, Kelly?'"

At that moment, her mother snatches her hand from me, her cheeks bright red.

"Come on, Charlie, let's go," she murmurs as she drags her away.

"I don't know why you're mad! You said he was nice!"

I tuck the card into my pocket, hoping that Katie doesn't see it as she walks over to me with her no-nonsense face on.

"What the hell was that about?"

My fingers nervously twitch over the card, hoping she doesn't demand to see it. I can't imagine what it says, but it will be far too personal, like something from a lover, not a stranger.

"Guys are finding creative ways to pass off their numbers, that's all." This lie is an insult to me as much as it is to her. I don't have his number, and I never will. My mystery stalker finds me when he wants and contacts me when he wants. I'll see him when he wants. He couldn't be more clear.

"So what's actually been going on? We both know you love abnormal psych, and the final should be no sweat for you. You've been studying. You know the material." The concern in her voice turns my stomach with guilt.

The truth is, I've been lying to her for a long time now, and longer if you count the months I suspected someone might be following me but wasn't sure. I know I have a stalker, but what do I do about it if I'm not sure I want him to go away? His note burns red hot in my pocket. It's one of many, and each one has chipped away at my defenses.

"It's just, starting this whole new phase of our lives and how much everything is about to change for us. It's only five months, Katie." This is an outright lie, and I hate it. "I'm worried about finishing at the top of our class. I've been pushing myself too hard."

That's what my mom says anyway, and parroting her nagging comes too easily, but the top spot is locked up, and we both know it. I've been desperate and hungry since the day we met. Katie knows I won't risk avoiding the life I came from by slacking off, and I won't pay to leave it by marrying a bastard like my mother did.

"Okay, Bianca. Whatever you say." It's clear she doesn't believe me, but more kids are looking to meet Santa.

I work the rest of my shift, and my stalker's eyes remain on me. I don't need any other messages from children to feel his gaze like the weight of a touch. He knows I haven't read his note, and his impatience courses through us both. Christmas lights flash from all directions, and boughs of holly and mistletoe hang in the air.

Read it, Bianca. Read it. I feel and ignore his demand, but eventually, he gives up, and that weight fades. He's off to wherever he goes when he's not with me… to the other side of the world, for all I know.

The time passes much quicker without anyone but Ralph paying special attention to me. I'm thinking about my stalker like usual and wondering what he looks like. That little girl saw him, but I was too shocked to ask. Why didn't I make her point him out? At least describe him?

We're closed for the night before I know it. Ralph takes off immediately, not offering to help with closing as normal. He pulls a fifth of Jack out of his bag as he goes. I would tell him to wait until he gets home, but he won't listen. Merry drunk driving Christmas.

Katie and I clean and pack everything away for the next day, but we still need about three hundred freaking goody bags put together and tied off. We could leave it, but I don't work tomorrow, and Katie does. I'd feel guilty leaving it on her to take the blame.

I pull out the supplies as Katie finishes with the mop, and her phone buzzes with a text. I should have started this an hour ago, but my thoughts have kept me so distracted.

"Bianca, my mom is here. Do you want me to stay and help finish up? I can tell her to wait."

"No, I'm fine here. Don't make your mom wait. She's already worked all day."

Katie nods gratefully and heads out. She's the oldest of six, and her mom has her hands full since their dad left. I watch as Katie leaves through the entrance near the food court, the door closing slowly behind her.

The mall entrances all open from the inside. So you can leave after closing, but no one can get in without a key, and regular employees don't have one. There are definitely other employees left in some of the stores, but none I can see. I'm feeling incredibly alone and nervous. My skin itches like I'm being watched, but he's been gone for hours.

I hurry as the adrenaline sets in, and my hands shake. I've done about fifty when I decide this isn't worth it. That's enough to get them started tomorrow morning, and Katie can finish the rest in the afternoon. She won't be pissed if I text her.

The note feels heavy in my pocket. I want to read it, but I need to be alone with his words. Each time I get one, I'm frightened. I'm terrified that this person watches me, follows me, and makes plans for our life together without my input or consent.

If my feelings on the subject stopped there, my only problem would be contacting the authorities and hunting him down. But then comes the warmth and indescribable satisfaction found in being the center of someone's universe. I've never been that before, and honestly? Being afraid makes me fucking wet. My hands only shake harder as I put everything away.

Twenty minutes later, I'm settled up. With my keys firmly

gripped in one hand, my other hand trails the letter in my pocket, and I'm ready for this day to be over. I close the door to the stand behind me, flip the little latch, and lock it as if someone couldn't easily hop over the divider if they wanted. I'm achy and missing the man I've never seen before, planning to fuck myself to his letter because they're always panty melters.

"Why didn't you read it, Snowflake?"

I stop dead in my tracks but don't dare look over my shoulder. I've only heard his voice two other times, so this makes number three. The deep, smooth, and hair-raising timbre makes me instantly wet. I'm overwhelmed by the instinctual feeling of being the prey. Being an inch from death charges me with the sweetest anticipation, the slutty neighbor of life-saving dread.

He's never said anything to indicate he means to harm me, but he's clearly not stable. He's never approached me directly before, and I'm struck by the realization that I'm not safe. This is a break from his pattern, and that means he's unpredictable.

"I asked you a question."

I turn, expecting to come face-to-face with him for the first time, but instead, I find a mammoth frame. Combat boots, black jeans, a thick red hoodie pulled up, and instead of a face to the letters, I find a full black plastic mask covering every identifying feature. The only things revealed are a flash of deep red hair and his bright green eyes through the openings.

I swallow a few times, trying to convince my brain to come up with words.

"I—"

He steps forward, and I shuffle back. I put up my hands, begging for mercy when everything about his appearance screams he has none.

"I usually wait until I'm home to read them."

"You always at least peek, Bianca. This time, you didn't."

Another step forward, and the urge to run rises sharply.

"I'm sorry."

"What if it was important? A matter of life or death?"

"Aren't they all?" I don't think before I speak, but I see his smile in the crinkle around his eyes. They're all I can see of his face.

"You really are such a good girl. It's a shame I have to punish you."

And with that, I turn and run for my fucking life. As much as I like his obsession and his attention, this is the first time he's mentioned punishments, and I'm not game to see what ignoring him will cost me.

CHAPTER 2
BIANCA

MY FREAKING ELF shoes slap on the tile as I sprint away, and the small bells on the tips of the exaggerated toes jingle with every step. The snap holding my thigh-high candy cane socks pops off on the right side. The one begins to slip, and I pray it stays in place and doesn't send me sprawling while a giant masked man is hot on my trail.

I dodge around Santa's Village, hanging onto a pole decorated like a candy cane to give myself an extra jolt of speed as I take off toward the major department store and my car.

Hiding is out since my frantic escape is less than quiet. His being at least six-foot-five and built puts a real damper on the idea of me fighting him. I'm not against it if I have no choice. In fact, it sounds kind of hot, even if I'm sure it would end in my death. Realistically, my best bet is to outrun him. I'm not fit, and my outfit works against me, but I'm pretty certain he'll strangle me and fuck my corpse for ignoring him, so it's time to kick my ass into high gear.

He's never ignored you, my subconscious snipes as I pump my arms harder, and my lungs burn.

Not a healthy thought to have, Bianca. He's your stalker.

I run as fast as I can, looking for someone or something

that can help me. The stores are a blur, and I start to realize I'm here a lot later than I thought. I might actually be alone. My lungs scream. He's too close to me. I know it even without looking.

"Bianca," he sing-songs behind me, taunting me. My name on his lips has my feet catching under me, and I nearly trip. Instead, I push myself even faster, the obnoxious bells on my toes picking up the tempo.

"This is silly. We both know your ankle has to be sore after being on your feet all day."

I look over my shoulder at that, finding him only about ten paces behind me. How the fuck does he know every single thing? Like the fact I broke my ankle playing basketball in sixth grade, and it's never been right since. He barely sounds winded, and I'm half dead from the effort. Plus, he's absolutely right. My ankle is killing me. He's playing with me.

"Be my good girl and take your punishment. I'll rub it for you."

That doesn't sound like someone trying to kill me, but he could be luring me into a trap. He's pissed. I can feel it. Violence practically pours off him, but I think I have a chance to get away.

Until I don't.

He lunges, his hand closing around one of my braids and yanking my head to the side, but ultimately slipping as I push forward. He's still on me, and I scream at the pain and pure primal terror. The only option left is the doors to the parking lot, but if no one has seen us yet, my chances out there are only that much worse.

At the last moment, I realize that while the lights are off, the metal gate on the major department store is only half down. I dash to the right and through the partially dropped gate covering the wide opening. My scalp screams as I roll across the tile and regain my footing on the opposite side.

A loud bang, then a curse as he crashes into the metal gate, trying to catch me, not realizing what I was doing when I darted right. I don't know the toy department all that well as I take off into the dense racks. I have a little bit of a lead on him, so I pause long enough to kick off my ridiculous shoes and keep running, this time at a full sprint that puts a lot more distance between us.

"That was a stupid move, Snowflake, and you'll pay for it." He groans and kicks the metal. The bang and shaking echo through the empty store, and I swallow a shriek, but I can tell he's far enough away for me to have hope of escaping. Someone has to be here, maybe in the storeroom. I turn perpendicular to the direction he saw me run and continue along the wall.

I'm about to cross into women's holiday sweaters when I see a door marked staff only. Checking behind me, I don't think the behemoth of a man knows where I've gone. I take the opportunity to slip inside, considering it a holiday miracle that the door is open, and lock it behind me.

I hold the knob for a minute as I force myself to take deep breaths. I'm not a runner, and the oxygen in my lungs feels thin like I can't get enough of it. "It's okay," I lie. "I've bought myself some time. This place is huge. He won't find me."

Time to hide. I turn, hoping to find a large box or perhaps a closet I can pull something in front of, when I realize this isn't some store room. It's the access for the mall's most elaborate Christmas window display. The animatronics are turned off and so are most of the lights, but the entire mall is set out in front of me. The fountain splashes, the color set to red for the holidays. The escalator stands still.

I pull my phone out of my pocket. I'm going to call mall security to get me the hell out of here. I won't call the police for reasons I don't want to examine too closely. I'm surrounded by thick hanging garlands, and mountains of cotton fluff beneath my feet. The phone rings three times before the door crashes open, the wood splintering and flying everywhere.

I scream as he pulls his body through, not bothering to remove the splintered wood tearing at him in his desperation to get to me. That violence I feared is a separate presence in the room, and I'm entirely cowed by it.

Backing into the wall of oversized plastic ornaments, I kick an oversized plastic candy cane and trip in the same step, crashing to the ground and crushing empty boxes wrapped like presents beneath me. The position I find myself in is revealing, and I try to shove my skirt between my legs to cover myself.

His red hood is still up, his rigid plastic mask still in place. The only hint he's furious with me is the tightening around his eyes. He looks like a dark rendition of Santa surrounded by all these decorations, a well-dressed model placed here to sell modern clothes along with the holiday cheer. I'm fucking wet for him already, and I'm pretty sure he's going to kill me.

"So help me God, Snowflake, if you called the cops on me." I hold the phone dumbly but say nothing, looking up at him. A voice echoes through the line, saying hello. "Is that 911?" he repeats, fury radiating off him.

"No, just mall security." I end the call and drop the phone beside me. His laughter is outraged rather than amused.

"You're fucking crazy if you think mall security could do a thing to keep me from you."

"Could the police?" I try to push myself into a more dignified position but slip on the cotton snow.

"They have guns, so they could kill me."

But he's not worried about that. I'm on the ground, legs slightly spread, too fucking shocked to even snap my knees together.

"Open it," he spits.

My legs for you?

"What?" My fingers dig through the mountains of cotton fluff I landed on top of.

"Open the fucking letter, Bianca."

Shaking, I arch my body and reach into the pocket sewn into the inside of my skirt. I pull out the crumpled envelope and examine the cream letterhead, the steady calligraphy *KS*.

> *Snowflake,*
>
> *I hope you're having a good shift. I know you're a good girl and haven't done it on purpose, but I need you to be more careful with what belongs to me. Your skirt keeps getting stuck, and while I enjoy you flashing me your ass and cunt, I doubt that pervy fuck behind you is your intended audience.*
>
> *Klaus*

What's Klaus's last name? The paper shakes in my hand as I read it twice.

"Nothing to say?"

I swallow, surprised by how fucking embarrassed I am. I wasn't expecting this. "I wasn't doing it on purpose." In fact, I was already upset and embarrassed by Ralph's attention. I did not want to encourage it, and did Katie really not notice if he did?

He doesn't respond. It's stupid to defend myself when he's already written that he assumes the best of me. That single thought is such a deep relief to a broken part of my soul I nearly choke on tears.

"My messages aren't meant for you to ignore, Snowflake. I watch out for you for a reason. You need me."

"I've been fine on my own for a long time, Klaus." It's the first time I've said his name out loud.

His eyes close, and his fists clench like he's savoring the experience.

"You have no idea how long I've been around to help you, Snowflake. It's not for you to decide which of my messages get priority. They are all of immediate importance to you. Do you understand me?" His voice shakes, and self-preservation tells me to be quiet, but I've never listened to my own good advice.

"What is there to understand? You send me letters. I open them. You tell me how you're going to fuck me, how we're going to live one day, and I have no control. I have no access to you, but I'm open to you. Isn't that the game?"

He walks forward until he's standing above me, and I have no more hopes of escaping. His booted foot is the length of my whole stomach, and I think how stupid I am to say anything when he could so easily stomp me to death.

"This isn't a game for me, Snowflake. This is about our future. Everything I've done, I've done for a reason. But if you want to play games so badly, we can arrange that before your punishment."

He flicks the switch on the display I'm leaning against, and suddenly, we're surrounded by lights, music, and animatronics in their full swing. "Rudolph, the Red-Nosed Reindeer" plays, and a train full of fake presents pulls past us.

"Festive, huh?"

I flip over and try to scramble away, but he snaps his legs together around me, his boots on either side pressing into my ribs and holding me in place. A fucking snowman waves at me as Klaus bends and grabs me by my braids. He wraps them each around his fist before twisting my head until I see him over my shoulder.

"You're mine, Snowflake. Every fucking thing I am is yours. Do you really think you don't have access to me? I'm always watching. Open your mouth and say my name, and I'll find you."

"How?" I demand breathlessly.

"Well, that would be telling, and I prefer keeping you a believer."

He shifts his feet, pulling me up by my braids. I groan at the pain ripping along my scalp but quickly shoot out my palms to take the worst of the pressure. He doesn't stop, dragging me all the way to my feet.

Once I stand, he spins me by my braids until I face him. From his deft handling, I get the impression he's done this before. His eyes crinkle in a smile as they drag over my body. Barefoot, costume askew. He yanks, pulling me up on my toes until I'm barely able to stand, and I hang onto his arm to keep from falling over or dangling by my braids. I feel beyond tiny as I cling to him, practically begging him not to destroy me.

I look up through our arms, past the pain in my scalp, and meet his gaze. He stares back, and it's the first time I've ever been so close to him or seen him in any real way.

"Feel that, Bianca?" he asks, and fuck me, I do. Our connection is soul shaking.

He leaves me on the tips of my toes as his free hand explores my body. Starting with my open lips, he slides down my neck and over my shoulder. He pinches my nipples through the costume, and I moan, still hanging on for dear life, but his green eyes drill relentlessly into mine.

"It's been a long time since I've been this close to you while you were awake."

"I know you?" I don't bother to comment on the fact he's been this close to me when I wasn't conscious. I should feel violated, but my pussy twinges desperately at the thought.

"You wouldn't remember me, pretty Bianca, but yes. You've been mine for a very long time now."

His words leave me reeling, flipping through anyone I could possibly have known with that hair. It's such a deep red compared to the more standard orangey hue. Just like he said, I come up blank.

His fingers slip beneath the waistband of my skirt, and my eyes roll back as chills break out along my skin. Oh God, his touch is… He smiles when he finds the trimmed but very present hair on my pussy.

"Do you keep it this way on purpose?"

"Yes." Why am I nervous about his reaction? For fuck's sake, I should kick him in the balls and try to run. Is being bald that big of a deal? He doesn't comment further as his fingers slip down, finding my pussy lips already swollen and leaking my arousal.

"Sleigh bells ring, are you listening? Pretty cunt so wet it's glistening." He sings his own version of the song as the track changes to the next on the preprogrammed playlist. His deep, silky laughter rumbles through his chest as he plays with my pussy lips.

"You're hilarious."

"Just in the spirit." He nods around us to the decor. "You seem tense, Snowflake. For someone in the holiday business, you seem awfully bah humbug."

"What are you doing?" I ask, but God, don't I know. My clit swells in the hopes of pushing past my lips and meeting his trailing fingers.

"You need this, Snowflake, just relax."

"And if I tell you to stop?"

He stills for half a second before he gives in to my eager clit and applies glorious pressure.

"Tell me to stop and see what happens," he taunts.

A single thick finger works my clit up and down, the sensation just enough to make me desperate. My pussy clenches on nothing, needing to wrap around something thick and hard to come. That same animal part in my brain urging me to run has already been activated and now begs me to fulfill a different instinct.

"Tell me to stop, Bianca." Green eyes like pine trees hold me hostage more than his grip.

He rubs my clit until I whine, "Please don't."

Klaus pulls his hand away from my pussy, and I shudder at the loss. My hips mindlessly try to find their way back to the stimulation. He reaches behind me with one hand, unceremoniously ripping a piece of garland from the display. He shifts my braids out of the way as he drapes the garland around my neck and doubles it over like a scarf. It's gentle and tickling in a way that makes me shake. I laugh manically as he drags the length over a particularly sensitive spot.

Then he pulls it tight.

My laughter cuts off in my throat, and my hands fly to my neck, trying to loosen the ligature, but he only squeezes tighter.

"You feel that, Bianca? That's how I feel when other people get to look at what's mine and get hard for what's mine. I can't fucking breathe."

My eyes burn, and my mouth opens as I seek air. His mask presses against my nose and my lips. It's close to a kiss but much too aggressive, too full of the anger and punishment he promised.

It hurts, and I would whine if I could, but instead, I gag brokenly. Was I really flashing Ralph my ass and pussy? I'd be embarrassed if I had room for anything but terror and arousal and a need to survive.

"But he's never going to fucking look at you again."

Is that because Klaus is going to kill me? My consciousness slips. Then things go fuzzy. Gasping, swirls of color, complete fucking euphoria. I come back to him with my face pressed against his mask, my spit smeared across it. My legs dangle for a moment before he sweeps my knees out from under me with the arm that isn't holding the garland around my throat.

He carries me across the room, and I cling to him desperately as he does almost nothing to support my weight and keep the pressure off my neck, but my arms are shaking and weak. The high is hard to fight. He drops me in front of the animatronic Santa and shoves my face into his lap. The thing's texture is surprisingly realistic, and unlike the others, he isn't waving. This thing must be kept in a barn. It fucking reeks.

Klaus kneels behind me, pushing my skirt up. Every other part of my outfit is in place but my panties, which he rips. His fingers are back sliding through my wetness, and suddenly, I don't care so much where my face is.

"You want Santa to see your cunt so badly? Let him watch while I use it."

I miss his pants unzipping through the light-headed buzzing, but suddenly, the hot flesh of the head of his cock presses against my entrance. That's a lot wider than I expected. My lips stretch, trying to wrap around him, but every part of him is so much bigger than me.

I shout as he shoves that thing through my pussy's resistance and deep inside me in one thrust. The pain is momentarily blinding. I have this crazy thought that in the days before modern medicine, I'd definitely die if this behemoth impregnated me. His large hand rubs my back for a minute, easing me through his rough thrusts.

"Sorry, Snowflake, waited long enough. Need to feel you, fill you up with cum. Going to fill you with so much cum."

He's deep inside me now, the soothing circles in my back forgotten as his hand roams my body. That incredible euphoria continues to pulse behind my eyes, strengthening as he tightens the garland and brings me back to the edge. My pussy grips him, desperately trying to suck him deeper, while my conscious mind hasn't had time to make any kind of decision about whether I want to get fucked.

He traces my spine down the crack of my ass and stops just as the flesh meets my pussy. Spreading me wide with his thumb firmly placed in the tender spot at the juncture, he lazily cracks me open like a book. The pain of his grip is immediately overshadowed by the depth and strength of his strokes.

"I didn't want our first time to be like this, Bianca. I'm sorry." He doesn't slow. He doesn't release the garland from my neck. He holds it like a leash as he pummels into me. "Told myself I could be soft and romantic, but I like you choking while your cunt chokes me."

"Please," I manage, but I'm not sure what I'm begging for.

"Shh, baby. You're going to come." He tightens the garland, bringing me back to the precipice of passing out all too quickly. Deft fingers reach around to find my clit. I lose consciousness for a second time and wake up screaming as my cum drips over his balls and down our legs. He grunts in my ear, my body still pulsing as he finds his orgasm inside me. His cum is hot and soothes this neediness I didn't know I had.

"Take off the mask, please," I beg as he slaps his hips against mine, finding the last pulls of his pleasure from my eager pussy. I slam my hips back against his, wanting every drop.

Five more pumps, then he slides out of me. I look back over my shoulder for him, black mask still in place, but now his hoodie has fallen, and his thick dark red hair is exposed. I always imagined it black or brown, but he's special.

"You don't really want that, Snowflake." He strokes my back. "Don't worry, you'll see me soon enough." He touches my face, and my eyes fall shut on a satisfied moan.

Real lips press against my temple for the briefest second, and I try to turn toward his exposed face, but a prick bites into my neck, and everything goes black. Not fuzzy, weightless, or high, just drugged emptiness.

When I wake, I'm in my apartment, lying naked in my bed. There's a note beneath my hand and a sore, wet feeling between my legs. I reach a hand into my panties and pull out a mix of both our cum.

Oh fuck, he really finished inside me.

I stretch, roll out my joints, and note with surprise my ankle isn't as sore as I expect it to be. I look down, and it's propped up on a pillow. Did he rub my injury for me after he choked, fucked, and drugged me?

I turn the paper over and check the message right away. Like he said, it's not up to me to decide how important they are.

Get your affairs in order and drink plenty of water, Snowflake. Christmas Eve, you're mine.

Klaus

I look over to find my elf costume and the shoes I ditched while running from him neatly piled in the corner. They're wrapped in a bag like they've been dry-cleaned.

CHAPTER 3
BIANCA

I BREW a pot of coffee and try to be quiet enough not to wake my roommate, Gina, who is an absolute bitch in the morning. My textbook sits on the counter, and I'm going over a subject that has been hot on my mind lately—personality disorders. There has to be a reason Klaus is doing all this beyond my magic Christmas pussy.

I run the water for the pot and hold my breath for a minute. Our apartment is a shoebox intended for college students and barely held together by super glue and duct tape. The walls are paper thin, and I've been yelled at for running the sink too long and too loudly in the morning.

Gina really is something, but after three years together, I'm used to her attitude. At least she always has her half of the bills on time and doesn't steal my food. That's an improvement from my past experiences.

I briefly consider waking her to ask if she saw how I got home last night, but that's like waking a sleeping baby. You just don't. She's as paranoid as she is cantankerous, so we don't have security cameras either. She doesn't want to be watched. A part of me thinks it would be better to live alone, but with Klaus watching me, maybe not.

My favorite mug is already half filled with cream and sugar. I'm just waiting for the pot to finish brewing so I can turn it a light barely coffee color. I have a bit of a sweet tooth, and I love the cookie selection that comes with this time of year. The comforting scent of coffee and gingerbread fills the air. I'm a sucker for the holiday flavors. But before the pot finishes, my phone rings.

That's weird. Who calls at seven thirty?

I head down the hall and back to my room so I don't accidentally wake Gina before clicking accept and pressing it to my ear.

"Hello?"

"Is this Bianca Rossi?" a loud male voice asks. It's definitely not Klaus, and I admit I'm disappointed. He's never called before, but he's also never fucked me senseless or choked me unconscious. So there's a first time for everything. Last night was insane, intense, and the best experience of my life. Bruises ring my neck, and I swear I just want him to add more.

"This is she," I answer, still not concerned, assuming it's someone from the university.

"This is Detective Adams from Center City PD."

That pulls me up short. Oh God, I hope my mom isn't hurt. Kevin hasn't sent her to the hospital in years, but... I try to keep calm.

"What can I help you with, Detective?"

"There's been an incident down at Center City Mall."

I sit down on my bed, relief washing through me before anxiety once again grips my bruised throat.

"The mall?"

"I'm going to need you to come down here and answer some questions. I'm posted in the security office while we conduct our investigation."

I don't say anything, the events I can remember from the night before running through my mind. What are they investigating? The damage to the display? That seems like overkill.

"Is that a problem, Miss Rossi?"

Oh God, there's video. Of course there's video. My throat sticks to itself, and tears well in my eyes. It's bad enough that I didn't consent to what happened, and I fucking loved every second of it, but now I have to somehow justify my lack of boundaries to other people.

"I'm sorry, why?" I sound very far from normal.

"Listen, Miss Rossi, this isn't something we can discuss over the phone. Should we come and get you and have this conversation at the station?" I swallow hard, forcing myself to act normal. I clear my throat.

"No, no of course not. I'll be there soon."

"Alright, Miss Rossi, do hurry."

I end the call and rush to get dressed. At the last moment, I remember to put on a turtleneck to cover the bruises ringing my neck. The ones that make me wet and tingly every time I think of them. I'm panting as I shove my feet into my boots. I slam the door as I go, forgetting all about being quiet.

"Shut the fuck up, Bianca!" my roommate shouts, her voice carrying into the hall.

"See you later!" I shout back. I'm going to pay for that.

I'm stepping into the parking lot when I remember he plunged a needle into my throat and knocked me out. I sure as Christmas didn't drive home. I'm about to pull out my phone and use my favorite rideshare when I see my little blue sedan parked in the usual spot.

Snow crunches beneath my black boots, reminding me of Klaus's weight on my lungs. As I approach, I'm half hoping he's there and waiting for me. I'm half terrified of the same thing.

The car is running, the windows scraped and meticulously brushed, the only car in the lot free from snow. I get inside, and it's *warm*. A little sprig of mistletoe hangs from the rearview mirror, white berries gleaming. It smells amazing. What on earth did he do?

He fucking choked you out and drugged you, Bianca. This is not romantic.

But for some reason, I don't believe myself.

A trademark letter waits for me on the dashboard. This one is fresh and immaculate. He must have left it this morning when he dropped off the car.

Not romantic, Bianca.

> *Sorry about the trouble, Snowflake.*
> *Remember when I said you didn't want to see my face yet?*
> *Well, I know you don't like to lie.*
> *Klaus*
> *P.s. I don't want a lot for Christmas, but your spread cunt will be underneath my Christmas tree.*

I smile so hard my cheeks hurt before I remember why I'm in the car so early, driving to the mall when I'm supposed to be off work for the day. I pull out of the spot and onto the side street leading to the highway. I'm too anxious to think about the coming conversation, so I run over the information I've spent years memorizing. School can't keep my focus, and I repeatedly drift back to green eyes, deep red hair, and a pussy-shattering cock.

Tomorrow is the twentieth, the day of my final, and the last day of the semester. I hate spending Christmas with my mom and stepdad, but that's the plan. It's too bad there's no way Klaus will get his wish. There's no way I could tell my mom I decided to spend the holiday with my stalker. She'd have me locked up.

The mall is only twelve minutes from my apartment, but the drive seems to take forever. Once I'm in the parking lot, I think about how to possibly explain what I know to be an assault that I truly enjoyed, wanted, and want more of. Talk about instant karma for thinking I could have my cake and eat it too.

I pick a spot near the swarm of police cars. That seems like overkill for a little public indecency. I turn off my car, open the door, and step out into the positively frigid air. The salt and sand on the parking lot crunch beneath my feet but don't entirely stop me from sliding on the occasional icy spots. Several officers pace the taped-off area, marking a crime scene. This definitely isn't about a little public indecency.

"Miss, the mall's closed." One of the officers stops me about ten feet back.

"I'm Bianca Rossi. I just got a call to come down here." He's a younger guy, and his expression tells me I'm expected. This can't be good. If I learned anything from my stepdad, cops knowing your name is a problem.

"Right this way," he answers immediately, directing me around the tape and into the building. Most of the lights are still off. The mall doesn't open until ten, and only a handful of stores with outside access can choose their own hours.

He leads us inside, past the window display where Klaus fucked me senseless. It's full of police officers and a couple of men with forensic kits taking samples of something. The officer turns to watch my face as confusion twists my expression.

"What the hell happened here?" There's no way they're taking samples of our cum, is there?

"Detective Adams was hoping you could help us figure that out."

Oh my God, what the hell did they see?

I follow the officer past the investigation and into the security office, where a portly detective with dark hair is taking up residence behind a desk that isn't his.

"Bianca Rossi," the cop escorting me announces.

"Miss Rossi, have a seat." The officer doesn't look at me right away, staring at something on the desk. My hands shake when I sit, and I try not to look too guilty. There's a camera if they want to see how I got fucked eight ways to Christmas, so I don't need to admit anything.

"What happened?"

"That's what I wanted to ask you. According to your coworker, you left here late last night, after most employees."

"That's true." But it sounds like he's asking. Why?

"The video footage is missing. Did you see anything suspicious?"

I blink rapidly. The video footage is missing. He hasn't seen what I've done. Katie told him I was one of the last people here last night, which is true. If they don't know I got screwed in that display, there's no way they're taking a bit of vandalism this seriously.

"Is someone hurt?"

"Someone is dead, Miss Rossi."

"Who?" My mouth hangs open, and a nasty suspicion rears up.

"Ralph Simpson." The Santa I've worked with these last six years. The one Klaus said was looking at my ass and pussy.

"Oh my God. What happened?"

"Please, Miss Rossi. I understand this is a shock, but I need to know anything you may have seen or heard before I tell you any details."

"I... I..." I take a deep breath. "I was distracted last night. I left late, and I was focused on getting to my car. I don't think I saw anything unusual. Ralph left more than an hour before me."

"The entire day is wiped from surveillance, but his car never left the parking lot.

"Did you see anyone or anything out of the ordinary, Miss Rossi? This is very important. Did you see his car when you left?"

"I had my headphones in." I'm such a fucking liar. I know exactly who killed Ralph. "I didn't see his car since we weren't parked near one another."

"That's a real shame."

"Why are they investigating the window display?"

He gives me a look like I'm being dense. "That's where he was found."

I gasp, and my genuine reaction thaws him.

"Whoever did this is a real sick son of a bitch. They propped him up in his chair, still dressed in his costume. We're just lucky one of the janitors found him before some kid. Six days before Christmas."

"Poor Ralph." I knew Klaus was dangerous, but this is so wildly far from what I expected. I thought he would kill me. I never thought he'd kill the people around me.

"I feel worse for his widow," he muses as he scratches at his beard.

"Can I go? I have a lot to do with finals."

"You can, but call me if you remember anything at all, Miss Rossi." He hands me a business card.

"I promise I will, but I really don't think I saw anything that can help you." *Liar, liar, liar.* "Wait a minute? Did you say that Ralph was found in Santa's chair in the display?"

"Yes. Does that mean something to you?"

Just that the lap my face was shoved into last night felt much more real than I expected of a holiday animatronic and smelled awful. *Let Santa watch while I fuck you.*

"No, it just seems especially cruel."

"I agree, Miss Rossi, but I need to get back to work." He dismisses me.

I leave the office scratching at my collar, feeling the bruises along my neck all the more poignantly as I walk past the spot he fucked me over a corpse. Not a friend necessarily, but someone I knew for years, and not just that, but he killed Ralph because of me.

I climb into my car, noticing the officers are all inside now, the tape still up. I close the door and stick the key in the ignition, but a hand tightens over my throat before I can turn it over.

"Don't scream, Snowflake." My eyes snap to the rearview mirror. He's wearing the same clothes from last night. It is the same mask, but the light blood splatter and dried spit marks are obvious. I don't think he's been home since his murder and what he did to me.

"I won't," I promise him. His grip loosens enough to let me breathe but remains possessively around my throat.

"Did you wash my cum out of that tight cunt?" My cheeks immediately turn bright red. I didn't even consider taking a shower once I got the call to come down and talk to Detective Adams.

"No. Did you clean ours off Ralph's dead body?"

His eyes crinkle.

"You're such a good girl for me, Snowflake."

I shake, terrified now that I know what he's done and where my face has been.

"And yes, you're safe. Like always when I'm around."

"Why did you do it?"

"You know why. You read my letter, eventually. Not before it was too late, though," he adds like it doesn't mean anything.

"I understand why you killed him. You made your point plenty clear last night, but why would you, you—"

"Do you really want an answer if you can't even ask the question?" I'm fucking amusing him.

"Why did you shove my face in a corpse's lap, Klaus?" He

smiles so wide I see the tops of his cheeks through the eye holes. How are those eyes even greener than I realized last night? So fucking pretty.

"I have a dark sense of humor, Snowflake, and I told you I would punish you."

I gasp my wordless outrage, briefly stealing all my thoughts.

"I thought you were going to spank me or something, not choke me and fuck me over a corpse."

"You would have liked a spanking, so how the fuck would that have taught you anything?" He's actually angry. I'm sure of it because he squeezes my throat tighter, and the action surprises him. "And you've learned now, haven't you? I don't have to do that to you again, do I?"

I swallow.

"Yes, I don't ignore you. Why haven't you asked me if I told them anything?"

"Why do you think I left the mask on? You could tell them whatever you wanted, and your conscience would be clear. Did you tell them how I used your tight cunt, baby?"

"And if I told them everything?"

His eyes grow serious but not angry. "You're still on my nice list, Snowflake. I know you didn't."

"How?"

"Because I've always known everything about you. Now stop asking questions." His hand tightens. "You're going to drive me out of here and officially become my accomplice."

"Or?"

"I'll choke you to death and make you come while you die." I start the engine and begin to pull out.

"And they say romance is dead."

His deep, smooth laughter rings out behind me.

"God, I'd love to fuck your throat right now, turn your cheeks as red as Santa's suit, but I have work to do to prepare for Christmas."

"About that, Klaus, I can't spend it with you." I don't tell him why since Ralph's blood is still splattered on his mask. He doesn't say anything for a minute, ominously holding my throat. I follow his directions exactly as he instructs, and his hand doesn't budge the whole time. I'm shaking with fear and arousal, and I wish more than anything he would tell me to pull over and fuck me again.

"Drop me at the next corner." I drive another half block, then stop the car. He releases my neck, leaving me strangely hollow.

Klaus gets out of the car and quickly darts to the other side of the street. At the last minute, he looks back, seeming to change his mind.

When he stomps back over to me, I roll my window down. An oversized hand reaches through, grabs my hair, and tips my head up. The other hand slides his mask just far enough to expose his full lips, and then they're on mine.

Fucking bliss.

CHAPTER 4
BIANCA

KATIE and I sit on her couch, wrapped in blankets, with the door to her apartment locked, bolted, and chained. Her place is a lot nicer than mine, in a building with security, and she has the best hot cocoa recipe passed down from her nana. We sip steaming mugs of it, and I lick the chilly whipped cream off the top as a delicious break from the terror and tragedy.

A Hallmark movie plays in the background, but neither one of us is really watching it, and the treat doesn't fill the empty spot in my chest. Whether it's from Klaus's absence or being fucked facedown on the corpse of a coworker, I don't know. I'm still sore all over. I'm not comfortable going home, and sleeping here is a relief, but I'm dreading bedtime. What if Katie asks me why I won't take off my sweater?

I don't bother to decorate most years, getting enough holiday cheer from the mall, but Katie loves it, and her tree is a little over the top for a single college student. Fat ribbons and candy canes, along with the standard lights and ornaments, hang off it. Boxes of leftover lights sit beside her kitchen counter. Who actually has more strands than they need? Garland hangs over her breakfast bar, and I can't help but blush.

"I really am sorry I involved you, Bee. I know how much you like your schedule. It must have thrown your whole study pattern off…" She looks pointedly toward the bag I haven't touched. "Are you going to be mad at yourself if you don't start now?"

I'm not. I've studied and know the material, but I lied to her last night when she asked me what was wrong. Then I got fucked by my stalker, who murdered my coworker.

"It's okay, Katie. You had to tell them I left after you because I did. And I didn't see anything. I couldn't help them." I've been lying so much lately, and while I'm used to keeping my secrets close, outright lying is different. Especially to Katie, who knows me better than anyone but Klaus, the murderer whose last name is still unknown.

I'm suddenly gripped with another terrifying realization. I don't even think that's his real name. He said I could have told them everything. Klaus might be common enough in Germany, but not here.

"I'm glad you're not upset. My nerves have been fried since I found out what happened to Ralph. We were in the mall with a murderer, Bee. It could have been anyone. That's terrifying."

"Klaus," I say his name out loud, feeling breathless. He said all I had to do was speak it, and he'd appear, but that can't be true. It's not even real. He's not even real.

"What'd you say?" she asks, but she really didn't hear me.

"Nothing, you're right. It could have been anyone. It's really scary." My final is tomorrow, and Katie's apartment is farther from school, but I'm too afraid to stay alone. Too wet at the idea of a fucking murderous stalker breaking into my apartment. No, I can't afford to be alone.

"I'm so sorry I didn't wait for you," she confesses, the weight of her words slumping her shoulders.

"What do you mean?" I turn to her and grab her hand.

"I should have just waited. What if something had happened to you?" Tears well in her eyes, and I realize what a profoundly terrible person I am. Not just to the people who loved Ralph but to my friend who is worried for me, who I'm lying to, and has every reason to be concerned.

"Nothing happened, Katie. I'm safe." Another lie. I'm so very far from safe.

"From what the detective said, it sounds like whatever this was, was personal and certainly did not involve me. I don't think we have a murderer rampaging through the mall on Christmas." I fucking know we do, and I've done nothing to help stop him.

"I know you're right, but I can't help it, Bee. You know I worry about you."

It's hard not to, given the state I was in when we met at thirteen. My mom had been married to Richard, my stepdad, for a year, and he'd been beating the crap out of me. My mother never did anything since he was beating her worse, but it stopped shortly after, and I still don't know why he stopped.

Katie doesn't really know the extent—she only thinks she knows. My mom isn't a bad person, but she's weak, and I hate going home. Richard hasn't touched me in years, but the memories and resentment haven't faded. I don't know if he's still hurting her. She keeps that kind of thing hidden.

"I'm fine, Katie. You know I can take care of myself."

"I just worry about how you take care of yourself." I choose not to answer that, and this time, I actually pay attention to the movie. She watches me for a few moments but eventually gives in and returns her focus to the movie too. The romantic holiday cheer barely scratches the surface of the tension in the room, but we eventually both fall asleep.

I wake to the soft twinkling light of the tree falling on my face, and at first, I think it's just my usual middle-of-the-night pee break, but then I realize what woke me is the gentle sensation of a hand slipping my shirt over my stomach. The other plays with an achingly hard nipple. My entire body is aroused, like he's been touching me for a while.

My clit pulses in tandem with my nipples, and I'm so fucking horny it's disgusting. For a moment, he doesn't realize I'm awake, and I'm too lazy and pliant to even think of fighting when I could practically come from how good his hands feel.

Then reality snaps in, and I jerk forward. He pinches my nipple, likely in surprise, and I open my mouth to scream. A strong hand slaps over my mouth from behind me. He's behind the couch Katie and I are sleeping on, but I feel his mammoth body all around me.

His body heat pours off him, along with the faint scent of pine and intense male pheromones. Chills break out over my body, and my nipples stand on end as his fingers dig into my cheeks, pressing firmly into my teeth. A whimper leaves my throat, and I fail to choke it down.

"You called for me, and I always hear you, Snowflake."

I don't scream or struggle, but I shake my head, denying the claim, my teeth cutting up the fine skin on my inner cheek from the pressure of his grip and the movement.

I didn't call for him, I've never. He's always been the one to come for me, but then I stop mid movement because I most certainly did say his name. How did he hear that when Katie, sitting beside me, didn't catch it?

"Keep quiet, or you'll have to explain my presence to your friend."

His hand slips from my mouth, and God, I do stay quiet because what the fuck would I say if Katie woke up right now?

"I never asked you to stay."

"Tell me to leave."

He already proved he's willing to kill, and the last thing I want is for her to get hurt when I don't even really want him gone. He doesn't have a weapon that I can see, and he hasn't threatened me. I have no good reason for not screaming other than the fact I'm already wet.

"You have the prettiest skin. Did you know that's why I call you Snowflake?" he growls in my ear, and I feel the plastic of a rigid mask against my skin. I shiver in fear and disgust at the thought of that same bloody, drool-covered mask touching my skin again. "I'm going to see every inch of it tonight."

He moves back to the hem of my shirt, pulling it up and over my head and arms. My black curls fall against my skin, and his hands straighten them before moving over my breasts. Katie shifts in her sleep only a foot away from me, and every inch of my body stiffens.

"It seems I want you afraid for all sorts of reasons."

He reaches behind me, unclipping my bra and letting my full breasts drop. The weight increases the ache in my nipples, and I bite my lip to keep from begging him to touch them again, but I don't need to. His fingers are on me, skillfully rubbing.

"You know this isn't the first time I've played with your nipples. I know you like it, watched you do it to yourself while you fucked your toys, and I couldn't help myself. But this is the first time I've touched them bare." Flames rip my body open. I'm fucked in the head because I'm desperate to know…

"What else did you do while I was sleeping?" I don't sound accusatory. I sound like the needy slut I am.

"Most of the time, I just made sure you were safe, watched you, imagined what you would look like if you opened those icy blue eyes and saw my fat cock inches from your face, fucking desperate to give you my cum."

"Did you?"

He laughs softly, seeing the question for exactly what it is —hope rather than fear.

"Not until last night, pretty Snowflake. We both felt you take my cum for the first time, and you didn't even wash it out of you until the next afternoon. Such a good fucking girl."

He watched me shower? How?

He winds something plastic and spiky around one wrist. It burns as he pulls it tight. I can just make out an unlit strand of Christmas lights in the muted light.

"Up."

"Why?" I'm suddenly more afraid of what he has planned than I am horny, if only slightly.

"Would you rather I milk you for your cum right next to your friend, leave you dripping down her couch? I've been pissed as hell I let your cum spill down my fucking jeans, but I'll waste some more to prove a point."

"Jesus Christ," I mutter, shocked by his mouth. I vaguely remember everything being incredibly wet as I came for him over Ralph's lap. *Shiver*. I was too high from the lack of oxygen to fully piece together what happened. I didn't know I could squirt before that, or until this moment really.

"On your feet, or you're coming right here."

I stand from the couch, and he moves with me. He's tall enough that my arm remains above me as I change positions. He stretches me up onto my toes just like he did the night before in the display, but this time, I have one arm loose. My leggings roll down my hips, and I try to keep them up with my free hand. My shoulder aches in protest, both already having been pushed farther than they're accustomed to last night.

"Such a good girl, Snowflake. So obedient for me. You know I'm a killer, and you still believe in me, don't you?"

The reminder sends a cold sting of terror through me.

"Please don't hurt me. I'll do anything if you don't hurt me." He steps around the couch, leading me over to the wall beside the Christmas tree. He doesn't hide from me, allowing me to see that while the mask is the same style, it's not the same one. It's a deep, deep red.

His eyes are crinkled in another smile, like he knows exactly what I was afraid of. His hoodie is a dark army green, locks of thick, deep red hair poke between the mask and hood, black jeans, and the same boots. Has he cleaned them, or are they still speckled in Ralph's blood?

"You just have to accept the reality that I want to hurt you, Snowflake, but if I hurt you too much, I don't get to keep playing with you." He laughs cruelly as he yanks me forward, and I stumble to catch my footing. "Now, now, we don't want to wake your friend." He says it like a mischievous taunt, like watching my embarrassment as we woke Katie would be just as entertaining as anything else he plans to do to me tonight.

My pussy spasms as I imagine the shock and horror on her face if she woke and caught me on his dick. Would she imagine what something that thick would feel like inside her? Would she wish she had a built stalker with a thick cock just for her? Fuck, I'm as bad as he is.

He pushes me against the wall beside the tree, only about twelve feet from where Katie sleeps. He drops to his knees in front of me and works my leggings down and over my feet, taking my panties with them.

"Squat."

"I'm sorry, what?"

He yanks my arm and applies pressure to my knees, forcing my forearm flush against my thigh. I'm squatting uncomfortably as he quickly binds my forearm to my thigh. He moves to the other side, and I nearly fall, but he grabs my foot, adjusting it until I'm at a ninety-degree angle, and then secures my other forearm to my thigh with a separate strand of lights. The bulbs dig into my skin at regular intervals, turning the bindings a little bit more painful. I whine, but I can't do anything other than wake up my friend.

"You fighting me last night was entertaining, but there's something delicious about you holding back for the sake of your dignity."

"Fuck you."

He widens my legs even farther, adjusting my stance until my back is against the wall and I'm effectively seated with nothing beneath me, arms bound to my thighs. I'm shaking already, stupidly weak. I don't work out, and I'm extra soft from the holiday cookies.

Once he has me exactly where he wants me, he moves to the wall, plugging all three of them in. The lights zip on with a slight electric hum. The colorful glow reflects off my pale skin, making me red, green, blue, and orange all over.

I'm spread wide open for him, needy and dripping, because his brand of fucked up is everything I need. I want to struggle and rip the lights out of the socket, but honestly, he's tied me really tightly, and I don't think I can. Plus, it would be a lot worse if Katie woke now and saw me wet and spread eagle for him ten feet away, glowing like a Christmas tree waiting to get stuffed like a stocking.

But he doesn't take his cock out like I expect. He lays on the ground beneath me and tucks his head under my seated body.

"Oh my God, what are you doing?"

"Eyes forward, Bianca. No cheating, or your friend over there will pay for it."

He removes the mask and rests it on his chest, and I keep my gaze directed straightforward. I'm not going to look at him, but I have the craziest urge to pick up the mask and put it on.

"Sit, Bianca."

"You can't be serious."

"Come on, that pretty pussy is desperate to get licked, and

your legs are shaking. No wonder I caught you so quick last night, baby. You're out of shape."

"No, I'll crush you." I don't even address the first part of his argument because he's not wrong.

"Don't care. Sit."

I don't answer this time, ignoring him in favor of focusing, using all my strength to hold myself in this position. But I'm not athletic, and I've never done squats, so I slip several inches.

"Don't tease a hungry man, Snowflake. It's not safe for anyone. Trust me, you'll be right here eventually." I try to stay up as hard as I can, but my legs literally shake and wobble like jelly as I drop another few inches. His hot breath teases my spread pussy lips as he laughs beneath me.

"Five, four…" The smug bastard counts down as the wobble increases.

"Three, two…"

I groan softly as I feel my muscles failing.

"On—"

My pussy silences him as my legs give out, and I drop onto his face as requested. His lips and tongue immediately get to work, devouring every inch of me. His nose tucks into my ass, and I think I might die of embarrassment for a moment before the intense sensations have a chance to catch up with my brain. I moan so long and low that I worry I'll wake Katie, but she only rolls away from us in her sleep.

His hands dig into my ass and thighs, rolling the flesh like he can't get enough of it, like he's just as hungry and desperate for me as he claims. His thick and wide tongue forcefully parts my lips, devours my clit, and eventually slips deep inside me to prod at my G-spot.

"Oh fuck," I whisper.

He props his hands under my ass, pushing me up and ultimately shaking some of the fear. I'm going to kill him.

"Come on, Snowflake, I'm thirsty. Come for me," he

demands before promptly dropping me back on his face and spearing me deep in my pussy with his tongue. One hand stays on my thigh, the other moves to my clit, stroking up and down as his tongue laps at me from the inside. I obey him because what else can I do? And I cry silently as my orgasm rips through me.

Actual tears drip down my cheeks as I try to stay quiet. Cum pours out of me, over his face, down his throat, over his chin. I watch the drips of my release slip over the blond five o'clock shadow on his neck. He moans as he licks me, doing his best to capitalize on my release and drink it all.

Eventually, the pleasure ebbs, and once again, he lifts me off him, this time sliding out from under me but staying close enough that my pussy is practically on his forehead. I don't look at him. The threat against Katie is enough to keep my eyes pointed at the Christmas decorations.

"Roll over, Bianca. Face in the carpet, ass up." He's breathless, coughing lightly like he inhaled some of my cum rather than drinking it.

"I can't move."

He reaches over his shoulders, grabs me by my hips, and tips me over. The way I'm tied, I naturally fall into the position he wanted with my cheek pressed against the floor. I hurt all over, and now that I've come, I feel every little ache and pain he's put me through tonight, but I don't need to want this. He's the one in charge, and my body has no intention of fighting him.

I'm already soaking wet and ready, and he enters me without any pause or preamble.

"This sweet cunt was made to take my cum. Feel how you stretch for me, Snowflake?"

"Yes." And I really fucking do. I never would have imagined all of that could fit inside me.

"Do you have any idea how good you taste?" He shoves

all the way into me, and I bite into the carpet rather than screaming and waking Katie.

"I asked you a question, Bianca."

"No," I murmur around the fibers.

He shoves his fingers between us, gathering my wetness, then reaches around to shove them in my mouth, pulling my face off the ground and risking being discovered.

"Delicious, right baby?"

I mean, it's okay. It doesn't taste bad, but the fact he thinks I taste that good? My pussy leaks around his cock. He hooks his finger into my cheek, pulling my face to the side and my mouth open. His hand rests on my lower back, and his hips slap against me. The mask is back in place, the red making him look even more like a demon than the black, and I think I'm going to come again.

"Oh, that's right," he comments as he feels the way I loosen and adjust for him. You're going to come again, aren't you, Bianca? Let's time this perfect, baby. Let you work the cum right out of me." He pumps a few more times, his breathing increasing and growing ragged. I'm getting close, but not close enough, when he releases my mouth and moves his spit-covered hand to my clit.

He rubs the bundle with my own saliva as lube, and in a perfectly timed movement, we're coming together. Breathing hard, we're trying to silence our grunts. My breaths heave into the carpet, and his face falls against my back as he squeezes my thigh so tight I nearly shout.

I don't squirt this time. My body is wrung dry, so his cum is wet and sticky between us. He pumps into me lazily a few times before he pulls out and watches his cum drip. He's upside down to me in this position, the center of my universe.

"It seems like a shame to cut you loose and leave you here when I could put another few loads in you, but I told you I have a lot of work to get done before Christmas Eve."

I consider telling him again I cannot spend Christmas with

him, but I keep my mouth shut. I got fucked, and as far as I know, no one died tonight. Despite not wanting to, he does just that, freeing me and helping me back into my clothes.

"Lock the door. I'll see you tomorrow."

"Will I see you?"

His eyes crinkle, revealing his smile. "Well, that would be telling."

CHAPTER 5
BIANCA

AT THREE O'CLOCK THE following day, I sit for the final. I've been using it as an excuse for everything. I'm not sure what I'll say to Katie now to explain my constant distraction and long glances. Hopefully, Ralph's murder will be enough to prevent her from asking questions, which only makes me feel even more guilty.

The test proves pretty damn hard, and I wish I did spend those last two nights studying instead of fucking Klaus, but as soon as I have the thought, my pussy twinges her boisterous disagreement. He's a murderer, he fucks me whether I approve or not, and I don't even know his real name. Yep, definitely great reasons to risk a lower GPA.

I'm done in the first hour and a half of the three available. Fifteen students have left before me, and forty-five remain. I mentally calculate what that means about how I scored, and like always, it doesn't actually tell me anything but gives me something to obsess over for a while.

I grab a sandwich from the cafeteria while on campus, and that feeling of being watched returns as I stop by the vending machine to buy some soda. I don't think Klaus will approach me. He's likely just watching me like he always does.

I'm completely fucked in the head, but his presence is comforting. I wish I knew which direction he was planted because I'd offer him a little wave, maybe bend over so he could enjoy my ass. I think better of that as I remember the reason Ralph met his untimely end and how many students here might also enjoy the show.

I'm pulling into the parking lot of my apartment building when I get a call from the general manager of Santa's Village at the mall. I'm not sure what I'm expecting from Carmen, but it sure as hell isn't her sounding pissed to the teeth.

"Bianca, where are you? Your shift started twenty minutes ago."

"What do you mean? Ralph is dead. There's no Santa." I'm too shocked to be gracious, and her disbelieving sigh follows down the phone.

"We replaced him. Get down here for your shift."

"You've already replaced him? Why didn't you call me?" My voice is quiet as I start the car and head to the mall, my costume already in my bag in the back.

"I replaced him that day. I just thought it was in bad taste to open before they could clean everything up, but we lost out on one of the most valuable days of the season. I didn't think I *had* to tell you to follow your schedule."

"Typically, no, but after my coworker is murdered, yes."

"Fine, fair point." She blows out some of her steam, her voice softening. "So get down here and help me make up for the lost sales, or we may not be opening next year."

I don't bother to tell her I wouldn't give half a crap, and I'm dying to be done with the Christmas industry permanently.

"Alright, I'm on my way. I won't be more than twenty minutes."

"Good." She's clearly not angry anymore. I've worked for her long enough and always been dependable. I'm not really surprised she's a morbid bitch of a capitalist, and at least I won't lose out on the hours.

"One thing, Bianca."

"Yeah?"

"The guy I hired is a little unusual. Don't stare, okay?"

"Why would I stare?" I ask aghast, assuming she means something is different about his appearance and that I don't have the social graces not to make him feel uncomfortable.

"He's... young." She seems to settle on the word. "Alright, Bianca. I'm covering for you until you arrive, so don't keep me waiting."

"Twenty minutes," I assure her as we end the call. I take the highway straight there and pull into the same spot as I did the day before when police were swarming the area. There are no police and no tape marking the crime scene. People bustle in and out of the mall, children in hand and strollers, arms overflowing with bags and wrapped boxes.

I walk through the door and see the display on my right. It's not exactly the same. A few things have been moved and new pieces added, but it doesn't look noticeably different. Certainly not like a man's corpse sat there for hours before being discovered just the day before yesterday, but I guess that's how life is.

A couple of minutes later, I emerge from the bathroom dressed as the same elf I've been for six years. Even though the costume is cleaner than it's ever been, thanks to Klaus, I feel dirty knowing what I did the last time I wore this—how and where I was fucked. I sniff the shoulder repeatedly, worried that I stink like sex and death despite knowing it's not possible. I stop off at a soap and perfume store and quickly spritz myself with a tester before carrying on my way, earning a dirty look from the girl working there.

"Apparently, Ralph liked cocaine, and the police have decided this was related to drugs or a debt, which Ralph also had plenty of." One of the girls who works at the froyo stands gossips on her phone as she walks past on her break.

That's just lovely, considering he's not even buried yet, says the girl who orgasmed over his dead body.

"Hey, Carmen," I greet my boss as I step through the gate into Santa's Village. A long line of mothers and children wait to see Santa. As she pointed out, these are the final and most important shopping days before Christmas, so not seeing Santa would devastate many kids.

"Oh, Bianca, good." Carmen can't stand children, and she's wearing her I'm-about-to-snap face as one of them grabs her leg. She passes the girl off to me, gestures toward Santa's chair, and says, "Bianca, this is Santa. I'm leaving." I escort the child back over to her mother who already holds a clear bag with pictures.

I glance up at my new coworker, at first seeing nothing wrong. He may be young, but he's wearing a puffy suit and beard. He's hugely tall, which may surprise people. His cap completely covers his hair and—green, green eyes, like pine needles, pierce me. My heart stops for a full second before picking up again.

He smiles, and I still can't see his full face with the damn beard on, but enough is visible to understand how utterly devastating my stalker is. How rocked I am to be in his presence unmasked after all this time. Why would someone like him pay attention to me? Women must throw themselves at him. Holy shit, this man is perfect, and he's been inside me, eaten my pussy, pressed my face into a corpse.

Impossibly green eyes cut across his olive-toned cheeks. He's still fair, but not how I typically imagine someone with red hair. I'm white like a sheet compared to him. Freckles scatter his cheeks, but not so many as to obstruct the view. They provide him with a false air of innocence, which is such an utter crock of shit.

Wide, sharp cheekbones, a half smile notching up his

cheek. I can't see his jaw now, but I remember it from when he kissed me, still covered in his victim's blood and my pussy. He's otherworldly, and just as Carmen asked me not to, I'm staring at Klaus.

"Bianca." She hisses, like this is the exact reaction she wanted to avoid, and it is, but she can't imagine why. "I'm leaving."

"Bye, Carmen," I force myself to say. "Hi, Santa." I can't tear my gaze away from him.

"Hi, Bianca," he answers in that all-too-familiar deep voice compared with the details of his face that are brand new. The way his tongue wraps around my name is just as sensual as when he shoved it inside me, and I'm wet and shaking. Terror for my safety and the safety of those around me wars with and fuels my arousal.

He watches my expression with a mischievous one of his own, so much like the look he gave me when he fucked me next to Katie the night before. Klaus is chaos, and I'm only starting to understand how deeply that runs and how turned on he is by his own destruction.

His eyes flick around the people as if to say, *Test me, Snowflake. I dare you.* But what does that tell me about his intentions for me and our audience? Why would he let me see him for the first time in public like this? His eyes meet mine. *I know it's tearing you apart. I'm enjoying it. Squirm.*

The next person in line steps up. The high school girl I'm working with tonight isn't a friend, not that we have any problems. We don't have anything in common, but at least I don't have to pretend with or explain shit to her.

She discusses the different packages with the mom while I grab the little boy's hand and lead him over to a literal fucking murderer. My knees knock together, clacking like an old cartoon, a teeth-chattering Christmas nightmare where I deliver a child victim to Krampus.

The little boy smiles at Klaus. He can't be more than four or five years old.

"Hi, Santa!"

Klaus looks over the boy's head to the watching mother, who mouths a name.

"Hello, Thomas!" Klaus booms, and the little boy jumps in excitement that Santa knows who he is. He climbs into his giant lap, looking oddly tiny cradled in it. Klaus patiently talks to him about what he'd like for Christmas and if he's tried hard to be a good boy. They decide together he could have behaved better, but he really tried his best. Next year will be better. Then they take their picture.

What. The. Fuck.

I'm staring slack-jawed when Klaus smiles at me. "Come on, Little Elf. We've got more customers." And we do. The line behind us is massive.

I keep working through the busiest shift I've seen so far. Carmen was right that a lot of people were upset over us being closed. I know this because they tell me, and the line stays dense throughout the night. I try not to stare at Klaus, but how am I supposed to reconcile someone so gentle and attentive to children is also a murderer.

At one point throughout the night, a man walks by a few times. I wouldn't have noticed him at all, except he keeps getting close to me, and once his toe stubs mine when it comes into the workshop. The next time, Klaus stands and calls him over to the booth.

I immediately start to tremble. Either he knows him and it's bad, or he doesn't know him and it's bad. They talk in whispers I don't have a chance of hearing, and I'm certain none of this will work out in my favor. The guy smiles, and they shake hands. Klaus returns to Santa's seat, and while his smile is bright, his eyes have a murderous glint.

Things slow down for a bit around seven, and we have a

fifteen-minute lull. Sarah plays on her phone, and I try to look anywhere but where I want to most.

"Bianca," he murmurs, and no one but me even notices he's speaking.

I shake my head, subtly denying him.

"Come here, Snowflake," he says, louder this time, and Sarah glances up from her phone but decides she doesn't care enough to pay attention.

I walk over to him to avoid the scene he's promising me he will make if I don't give in to what he wants.

"Why do you look so scared, sweetheart? I think this is going well."

"It is going well." I'm not facing him. Instead, I'm looking out over the mall despite only a foot separating us. He hears my hesitation, just like he hears everything else.

"Then why do you look so scared?"

"What are you going to do?"

"To you?"

"To the children." My voice shakes as I clarify my concern. Hours of fear and pent-up tension nearly bring me to tears. My eyes fill with them, but I swallow them down.

He's slower to smile this time. "Nothing, Snowflake. I like kids. Don't insult me again, or you'll pay for it." He reaches over and pinches the underside of my ass cheek hard. I squeak in pain, and he *tsks* when people look at us. He doesn't care what they see. He's simply mocking me.

When the shift ends, he's at my side, not giving me a chance to escape.

"We have plans tonight, Snowflake." His hand grips mine, and while it's not painful, I clearly get the message that he'll make it so if I struggle.

"I already had plans."

"With Katie? I took the liberty of canceling them for you. You're exhausted after everything that happened with Ralph and your final today. She's worried about you, but you'll pull through."

"How did you do that?"

"That would be telling, Snowflake, and I prefer to keep you a believer."

"Sarah, you can finish up here, can't you?" Klaus asks with his hand ever so lightly trailing my lower back. I don't know if she can see it, but she stares at how close he's standing to me.

"Yeah, I know how."

"Great. Bianca and I have plans with a friend."

"Uh, okay."

At that moment, the same guy who kept walking close to me, who stubbed my toe, pops around the corner and winks at Klaus. He pushes me along, and the guy takes the other side of me, crowding me in.

"Klaus, who is this?" The guy stands too close to me, and my skin crawls at his proximity.

"This? This is my new friend. What's your name, pal?"

The guy laughs a shitty, nasty sound. "Pete, nice to meet you, pretty lady." Chills break out on my skin, and not the good kind Klaus usually gives me. He reaches out a hand, and Klaus smacks it away.

"No touching yet, Petie. If you're too eager, you can't play."

What the fuck? I do not want this.

I try to get away from Klaus then, attempting to rip my wrist out of his grip, but he doesn't budge. He presses his mouth to my ear.

"Struggle and people will die. Maybe the children you're so concerned I'm going to hurt."

I stop fighting immediately and let Klaus and this disgusting creep beside me lead me out of the mall. I half expect him to push us over to my car, but instead, he leads us to a sleek Tesla.

"If you have this, why are you working as a mall Santa?" the guy asks in disbelief. Klaus pulls a device out of his pocket that is not the key, and the door opens.

"The tight pussy, obviously."

The guy laughs as he climbs into the passenger seat.

"Get in, Bianca." He pushes me toward the back seat.

"Please, Klaus. Please don't let this guy touch me. I only want you."

He pulls the stupid beard off, the hat too, and I see his face for the first time. My heart races, and my blood heats. Broad, artistic lips, a cut jaw, and the barest hint of a blond beard. Too perfect. Too evil.

"I'll do whatever the fuck I want with you. Now get in the fucking car." He speaks louder this time so the creep can hear, and his laughter chills my blood. I climb in the back seat, trying to stay as far away from both of them as possible, but the cabin is cramped, and they both feel like they're on top of me.

"Seat belt on, Snowflake." My cheeks are bright red, devastation and betrayal burn in my stomach, and I only obey him for fear of retribution.

The moment I'm strapped in, the guy reaches back to touch me.

"I told you not yet. You'll get a piece of her when we get there." Klaus pulls out a knife I didn't realize he had, and the guy immediately throws up his hands.

"Fine, man, fine, but I don't get why you're so possessive. I'm the one who scouted her."

Klaus says nothing, his jaw clenching. Despite whatever he plans to let this man do to me, he takes issue with the idea that someone else found me first. He's been following me since I was sixteen, that I know of. That's the first time I got one of his letters. He certainly has predatory dibs on me.

"Trust me, *friend*, I've been planning to have her since we were thirteen."

Thirteen? Is that when I met him? We're the same age? Who the hell is he?

"Fine, fine. Mind if I jerk off until we get there?" the man asks, already moving his hands to his pants.

"Yes, I absolutely fucking mind. Keep your cock in your pants, or I'll cut it off."

A tear drips down my cheek, and I wish I just fucking screamed the first night in the mall. Merry Christmas to me.

CHAPTER 6
KLAUS

WE PULL up outside Johnson's Tree Farm, family trees for four generations. The scumbag with the mirror taped to his shoes sits next to me with an obvious erection, and it takes all my self-control not to stab him in the dick right here for using that mirror to look up Bianca's skirt. I don't because he's not the only one learning a lesson tonight.

Their usual display and Christmas fair are all closed up, the last employee leaving promptly at eight thirty. The big wooden sign glows with the lights beneath it, and I slow down as I turn in and up the long, winding drive. I've been coming here since I was a kid, and so has Bianca.

I watch it on her face as she recognizes where we are, and I wonder if she remembers meeting me here all those years ago. I watch her face in the mirror. She doesn't. I shouldn't be surprised, but I am angry.

Old man Johnson hasn't been staying on the farm since he's been seeing the dairy farming widow two houses down, and I've made use of the farm and his house when I need to. It's one of the pros of not being real—someone without an identity, but also many. I'm whoever I need to be and have been ever since I realized I could never play a part in normal society.

I pull the car to a stop deep into the parking area where there isn't any chance of us being seen from the road. Bianca's breathing hard in the back, ratcheting up my tension and soothing the part of me that demands retribution. How dare she beg me not to hurt the children when I was doing everything I could to impress her? To prove to her how good I could be with them, how worthy I am. I'd never hurt children. They're honest, chaotic, and fun.

"Are you excited, Bianca?"

"Bianca, that's a pretty name." The passenger creep makes a sound close to a purr. I don't even have a cunt, and it closes up. I can't imagine how my Snowflake feels. Hopefully like questioning me in any capacity is a mistake.

"Fuck you, Klaus."

"Klaus, huh? Funny name for Santa. Don't worry, Sugar Cookie, we're going to fuck you plenty." Did he just nickname her?

That was a poor choice.

I crack open my door but don't bother to correct his misapprehension. He'll figure out he won't be touching her soon enough. A little sob from Bianca, an excited laugh of anticipation from the creep beside me. He thinks we're here to rape her. At least that's what I told him at the mall to get him to accompany us. He fucking agreed and shook my hand over it like a sick, greedy asshole with barely two sentences spoken.

I open her door. She scrambles away, kicking to escape. I take a couple of blows to my chest as I grab her by the upper arm and yank her out and onto her feet. I'm not angry with her for fighting. I'm proud of her for doing her best to only be fucked by me.

"This way, Snowflake."

I lead her through the darkened Christmas fair. The permanent sleigh stands in the center of the space with carved reindeer in the harnesses to pull the sled. It's a much more wholesome and familial scene than that gaudy window at the mall. I'm still wearing the Santa costume and my black combat boots. Snowflake is dressed like an elf, and the pervert's dick is so hard I'm surprised he hasn't creamed his Calvins.

I bend down as we cross beneath the entry arch to the small carousel and plug the lights in. The music kicks on, and the horses creak as they move. The whole place hums as flashes of color and Christmas shapes dance through the night air. The Christmas fair is fun, but of course the best part of the farm is the cut-your-own trees.

"This way," I tell them both as I lead them past the entertainment, dancing snowmen, and flashing candy canes and back to where they shove the trees through the mechanism and into the net. They're supposed to put the saws away at night, but they never do. The same is true for the axes, and I casually pick one up as we pass just far enough from the lights that it's harder to see for having them on.

"You know why he bumped into you, Bianca?"

She doesn't answer me, and I slowly swing the axe.

"He had a mirror taped to his shoe, and he was looking up your little green skirt at the tight pussy that belongs to me. Did you know that?" Again, she says nothing.

"Are we going to fuck this slut or what?" Pete interjects. "I'm so fucking horny, man. I'm going to blow before I get in her, and I didn't come all the way out here just to watch you get your dick wet." No, you certainly didn't.

My Snowflake is crying, and I regret waiting this long for my big reveal. Before he can finish his disgusting sentiment, I swing the axe over my shoulder and into his. The blade is heavy and dull. I know that objectively, but it feels like nothing to me as I use my superior height to cleave it into him. His shoulder separates from his body, hanging limply, and I rip the axe back out.

"Oh my God, Klaus! Oh my God!"

Snowflake screams in earnest now, and it's so fucking good to hear that she's as invested in all of this as I am. She's needed a good scream for days, and I've needed to hear it for years.

"Mine, mine, mine." I keep muttering as he falls to the ground, his moans and cries tearing up the night air.

"Why, man, why?" he wails as he tries to turn over and face me. He only gets a quarter of the way before I swing the axe into his chest. I rip it out, my body casting a shadow from the lights of the display behind us. Enjoying the sinister, festive visage, I swing again, and his blood splashes my face.

He falls back onto his chest, his effort to turn over as useless as his efforts to rape my Snowflake. The metal cleaves his back open as I swing again, thunking into his flesh with a thick, wet thud. Snowflake sobs, but if she's speaking words, I don't hear them.

I have only one goal. Rip, *shluck*, swing, cleave. I don't know exactly when he stops screaming, but it can't take long. My hands begin to burn as blisters strengthen my calluses. Bianca, on the other hand, keeps wailing long after he's dead.

I'm too fucking angry to stop chopping until he's nothing but little red pieces in the snow with Christmas lights twinkling over him like he's just another part of the decorations.

Dropping the axe, body heaving, ready to fight, fuck, something, I turn to Bianca, and she's staring at me like I'm a monster. She's right. I am. I'm going to fucking tear her apart. I step toward her, ready to grab her by her hair and use her body however I please over another goddamn corpse.

"Klaus, thank you for not letting him hurt me." That surprises me. She's shaking, but now that I'm looking closer, maybe she doesn't see me as a monster.

"He wanted to. He would have tried to rape you if I

wasn't there." Her gratitude slows my approach and takes the worst of my anger. Her pretty palms face me in surrender.

"He was looking up women's skirts?"

"Not just women, but teenage girls too." My jaw clenches, and my teeth grind.

"You look like you're about to hurt me." She spits the words, and I take the time to really look at her. I was too caught up in my kill, too high on the adrenaline to pay proper attention to her before.

Her round blue eyes are impossibly wide in terror, her pale, pale skin is nearly sickly, and her round red lips look bitten raw. I can't even spend too much time looking over her curvy body if I want a chance of paying attention to her needs rather than my own.

"Need to fuck you. Might hurt you," I answer, not back in my right mind. I'm still high on the feral chemicals that come with ending a life, with defending what belongs to me in a visceral, primal way. I need to fucking fill her with cum. It's a basic, biological instinct.

"Klaus, please. I'm already sore from the last two nights, and you're really scaring me right now. You're covered in blood, and, and—"

"That's not going to work for me, Bianca." I take another step toward her, not planning to stop this time. I am taking her. She shocks me by dropping to her knees, her hands rushing to take my cock out of the bright red Santa pants.

"I know you need to cum. Let me suck it out of you. Please, Klaus. Just not like this." She gestures to me, and I look over myself, seeing the blood she's referring to.

I'm half tempted to pick her back up, bend her over, and use whatever hole I damn well please, but I've dreamed of her eager mouth around me for years. She makes impossibly quick work of exposing me while I decide. Bianca has my cock in her hands, and it's hot and heavy, achingly cold where the night air touches it, and her hands can't manage to cover it all.

"Open your mouth right now and suck, so help me God."

She doesn't hesitate, taking me into her mouth, struggling with my girth. I put my hand in her hair and nudge my cock in until it's over her silken tongue and cresting the back of her throat. I'm covered in blood from head to toe, but my cock is clean, and now that I have the clarity of being inside her, I'm glad she's not covered in his likely diseased blood.

Her mouth wraps tight around my cock, her talented tongue struggling to work its way around the thick girth as she plays with the sensitive spots.

"Fuck," I grunt as I pump deeper, and she gags. Her fingers dig into my thighs as I push farther down her throat, taking her air. I give her a few minutes to acclimate. Use the time and pleasure to take the worst of my rage and excitement. Sinking that axe into that fucking bastard was only half the release I needed. I need Bianca.

"Hang on, Snowflake. You might pass out, but you won't die. I promise."

Her eyes flash with alarm as I shove as deep as I can, past the resistance of her throat, my cock thickening her neck itself. I grunt wordlessly at how fucking tight it is as she gags around me, but I hold my position. Her body tries to force her to retch, but my cock is too fat for her feeble struggles. Her pretty cheeks turn bright red like the lights flashing behind us as I use shallow thrusts to keep myself deep enough to choke her while providing the stimulation I need to finish.

I'm so close, a few more pumps. She's starting to turn purple, her eyes roll back as she passes out, and her throat goes slack around my cock. I fucking come, hot jets streaming down her throat, filling her, choking her.

Little broken gags come from her throat as she swallows, and my balls ache as they draw up and spill again and again. I could give her another few spurts, but I truly do not want to kill her, and she's nearly blue. So I pull back and let my dick twitch on her tongue while her body takes a moment to realize she can breathe.

When she still doesn't breathe, I smack her on the cheek with my dick, spreading the last leaking bits of cum from the side of her face to her lips. She takes a breath, choking, spluttering, coughing. I release her hair, and she drops to the ground at my feet. She's barely conscious, and from the smile on her face, vaguely high.

"Come on, Snowflake. On your feet." She doesn't respond. She just lies there, moaning weakly. "Fine." I sigh, throwing her over my shoulder and carrying her back to my car.

I don't bother hiding the body just like with the mall Santa before. They're all part of my happy holiday plans.

"See you for our shift on Christmas Eve, Snowflake," I tell her as I tip her into bed and place a kiss on her cum-flavored lips.

I leave her room and walk past her roommate again. She's watching me with hatred like she always does. She and I have been engaged in an odd truce for three years. She doesn't interfere, and I don't harm her.

"You should leave her alone. She's not a bad person."

"And who the fuck are you to make that decision?" She doesn't answer because she knows as well as I do that if she pushes it, the answer will be "a dead girl." "Merry Christmas, Gina. Don't become another lesson I need to teach Bianca."

"You need to stop killing them. How many is it now? Nine? Ten?" Her brown hair cuts off at her shoulders in weak, ugly waves. Nothing like Bianca's curls.

"You need to keep your mouth shut about things that aren't your fucking business."

"She'd hate you if she knew how many people are dead because of her."

"Good thing she doesn't need to know. She's safe. That's

what counts. Now stop watching me, or we're going to have problems."

"If we have problems, you have problems," she answers ominously as she heads back to her room. My little Snowflake has no idea what the people in her life are really like.

CHAPTER 7
BIANCA

I EXPECT to hear from Klaus the following day, but I don't. I don't have work until Christmas Eve, and he's all I can think about. I'm furious and shaken from what he did at the Christmas tree farm but oddly touched. Just like I am every time he does something over the top to prove nothing is more important in his world than me.

Someone at the Christmas tree farm must have called the police, but no one came to question me. I'm shaking and anxious anytime my phone goes off or there's a sound through the thin walls.

I text Katie that afternoon to ask if the new Santa came in, and she said:

> Yes, holy crap he's hot, and so good with the kids too. I think he has a little crush on you. Definitely go out with him!

He's there? Why the fuck is he there? That makes me even more nervous. The man is like a bomb about to go off, and now he's near my best friend and a ton of kids. But he was furious with me for suggesting that he would hurt children. I think that may actually be genuine since he hasn't felt the need to lie about any other aspect of himself. But making my best friend like him? That's low.

I expect to see him or hear from him that night, but I don't. Gina gets home from work a lot later than normal, and instead of running straight to her room to be antisocial, she lingers near the door.

"Gina, is something wrong?" I ask after about twenty minutes. She's not someone who likes to talk or be questioned, but the silence is a little much.

"I'm not planning to renew my side of the lease at the first of the year."

That's a shock, though it doesn't seem directly related to her hovering. But it's a kick in the ass because I need a roommate and finding someone for less than six months is hardly convenient.

"Can I ask why?" I expect her to tell me no and walk away, but for the first time in our three years of living together, she grabs a chair and sits across from me.

"Do you remember when we met?"

"Yeah, it was three years ago. You answered my flyer."

She stares deep into my eyes, and I see for the first time that she's not just confrontational, she's guilty.

"Don't find another roommate the same way. Ask a friend or family member. Find someone you *know*."

"Gina, what are you talking about? You're scaring me." I lean back on the couch, trying to distance myself from her like that will keep me from the truth.

"He asked me to stay here, to keep an eye on you. I-I... he paid me, but it's not right, and I won't do it anymore."

"He?" My body shakes. "Who is *he*, Gina?"

Brown eyes meet mine.

"You know who I mean, but I don't know who he really is either. Just that I've never been a college student, and I've never paid you rent. I decided you deserved the truth."

"After three years?"

"Yes. I never pretended I was a good person."

No, she absolutely did not.

She packs up her things and leaves that same night, but I still don't hear from Klaus, the murdering stalker who apparently hired my roommate to live with me three years ago.

Things are better and worse once I'm alone. Better because I shouldn't be excited to hear from my stalker, and I apparently was living with a plant for him. It's worse because I'm really excited to hear from my stalker, and I didn't mind his plant so much. I was kind of fond of her. I don't have work until Christmas Eve, but I'm hoping I get called in just to see if he keeps showing up to his shifts as fucking Santa Claus. If he's trying to fuck with my head, God is he succeeding.

The semester ending is a relief, but I worry my suddenly boring life isn't interesting enough for Klaus. Is that why I haven't seen him or felt his eyes on me? Is he watching someone else? And why does that idea fill me with burning jealousy rather than concern for that person? He's a fucking murderer and stalker, Bianca, not your boyfriend.

I find myself twitching instead of reading or watching whatever I put on TV. Rather than relaxing and enjoying the few free days I have, I'm counting down to Christmas Eve, my last shift at Santa's Village. Will he be there? I need him to be there. It's the end of an era after six years, and I don't even care about that.

That morning comes, and I get dressed in regular clothes before heading to the mall. I always change when I arrive, not just because the costume is uncomfortable but little kids like to stop and talk when you're walking around dressed like an elf.

When I walk into Santa's Village, Klaus is already seated on his red throne, seemingly waiting for me. He smiles that crooked smile, and I melt for him despite everything.

"Bianca."

"Santa," I answer, not wanting to disturb the magic for the children. He watches my face shift from relief at his presence to irritation. I don't want him to know how he affects me, but I can't help it. I'm pissed he's been gone. And other than here, where the fuck has he been? And why has he been here instead of with me?

He watches all that play across my face, and the satisfaction there answers my question. Axe murdering that man in the field wasn't the entirety of your lesson. Being ignored after is the other. It's hard to have our roles reversed, me being the one looking and waiting for him. I walk over to him and stand at his side, facing the line of children waiting to meet Santa. He's been my stalker for years, and he's suddenly the center of all our attention.

I paint a plastic smile on my face and talk through my teeth. "Do you have anything to say for yourself?" I can't help it. I sound like an angry girlfriend, not his victim in any real regard.

"Miss me, Snowflake?" His lips tip arrogantly beneath the curly white beard, and a little boy steps up to take his picture. He's too young to speak, so we both smile as the camera flashes.

"What if I said yes?"

His brows push together in surprise.

"I'd say I've missed you too." The little boy runs into his mother's arms, and I turn to sort out the goody bags for the next few children. "I'm sorry about costing you a roommate, by the way." His voice is low enough that I shouldn't hear it, but it always carries straight to me.

"Did she tell you she was quitting?"

"Yes, but I never stopped watching, Snowflake."

I don't answer him. I'm too angry. For one, I don't believe him, and for another, he's telling me he didn't stop stalking me to make me feel better.

"I'm not planning to stop paying your bills, so you don't need to worry about finding someone else to live with."

I'm fuming mad as I turn to face him, trying to block out how devastating his features are, or how deep that red hair is, how soft it must feel.

"Half the bills my hired roommate would pay if she wasn't a spy," I correct him because I've worked my ass off these past six years. He hasn't paid for anything. A few people look toward us, hearing the tone of our conversation but not the words.

Klaus smiles wide and waves to the children as he says, "She was never a spy, Snowflake. She was simply a dour deterrent for all types of company, and I have paid all your bills. You just don't know what I did with your rent yet. Consider me your savings account."

I stop with my hand on the drawer as another worker brings a child up to sit with Santa. What a miserable asshole. If he's telling the truth, where the fuck is my money, and who is he to pay my bills? And how the hell did he manage to find someone so effective for the task of keeping people away? Friends despised coming over to my place with Gina there, and she had cockblocked me on more than one occasion.

"I don't even know what to say to you right now." I'm so angry about so many things I could scream.

He fucking laughs.

"What's so goddamn funny?"

"I really didn't think I had an actual chance to win you over, but you're mad at me right now like I'm your boyfriend, and I think it's because you like me, Snowflake."

"Shut up."

"You do like me."

I turn my back on him to let more children into Santa's Village, and I must admit, I'm no longer afraid he's going to hurt them. I hate that he's right. He's won me over through two simple tactics, dogged loyalty a.k.a. obsession, and making me come harder than I thought was possible. To a forgotten girl like me, who's been lusted after plenty but never cherished? His attention destroys my defenses.

A few hours go by, and everything is within normal, allowing for a murdering ginger in his early twenties playing Santa Claus while I think about what he said to me the other day. He's proving himself worthy to me by being kind to all of these kids, and I hate to admit it's working.

I'm listening to an adorable conversation between Klaus and a nine-year-old boy who doesn't believe he's really Santa, when two women in their late teens or early twenties step up. For a moment, I'm confused, looking around for their children or siblings, but it's just them.

"Can I help you?" I ask pleasantly.

"We want a picture with Santa."

"Oh, um..." I want to argue, to tell them it's against the rules, but it's definitely not. This would be the highlight of Ralph's week if he wasn't dead.

"Sure, what package are you interested in?"

They both look toward Klaus and giggle.

"Uh, photo package," I correct.

"Whichever one is cheapest, we just want one picture for each of us."

"Sure." I walk away instead of leading them to him like I do with the kids. I'm sick in the strangest way, so jealous I could puke, and I'm wondering what the hell is wrong with me. I didn't even know I was a jealous person, but after the days of being ignored, the idea of him touching them is maddening.

They're laughing, and I look over my shoulder, expecting him to be staring at me mockingly or taunting me by flirting with them, but an all new pit forms in my stomach when I see he's genuinely distressed. The camera flashes, and I walk over to them slowly. The girls are unaware of anything amiss. They're peppering kisses on his cheeks, which is super inappropriate to do to someone at work who can't really tell you off, but his mammoth frame is locked in tension, his face turning red like he's not breathing.

"Hey, cutie. Is something wrong?" one of the girls asks.

The other rubs a hand down his chest to get him to talk.

"He's just shy."

I'm behind the chair, pretending to do something else. If they see me, they don't pay any particular attention, but I feel every bit of him practically begging for my interference. The pictures are done, and they don't stand. I knew this was an excuse to get a picture with the hot guy, but I didn't realize they were trying to pick him up.

He doesn't do anything to stop them, and I've had enough. I step around the chair, forcing them to pay attention to me.

"It's time to go. There's a line."

"Oh, we're just having fun with Santa," the one touching his chest teases.

"Come on, Hailey, there is a line." The other nods toward the kids and mothers, who are all watching with varying expressions of distaste.

They finally get off him, and the second they're no longer touching him, he drags in a deep breath like he stopped breathing entirely. His hands are on his legs, he's panting, then he stands and leaves.

I watch him go for one minute before I tell everyone Santa is taking a fifteen-minute break and run after him. I don't know exactly where he's headed, but I run in the direction I saw him go, and apparently straight past him since an arm comes out of a narrow hallway and pulls me in.

He shoves me against the wall, towering over me, crowding my space. Every inch of my body is hot with him and the damn fleece suit against me. The hat and beard are ripped off, and he's all wild red hair and incredibly soft lips. He still hasn't caught his breath, and something is seriously wrong. He presses his face to mine.

I place my hands against his cheeks, and he's hot. I kiss his lips on my own for the first time ever, but it's just a gentle press.

"No one but you," he murmurs as he shoves me back into the wall and turns the kiss into something deep and desperate.

"What do you mean?" He kisses across my cheek and down my neck.

"I don't want anyone to touch me but you."

I take a minute to absorb that, trying to understand what happened back there. "Hundreds of kids have touched you."

"I don't mind them. I like kids." Those same words suddenly seem unbearably genuine rather than taunting.

"Klaus, what's happening?"

He doesn't answer. I hold him as he shakes, and both of us sink to the floor. I think he's having a panic attack, and I think those two girls touching him were the trigger. So what the fuck is going on here? We sit in that hallway together, and by some miracle, no one finds us.

He calms down a while later and pulls me into his arms rather than me cradling him. It's the first truly tender moment between us, and it aches in contrast with everything else.

"I want to spend Christmas with you," I admit. "But I can't."

"Why not?"

"I have plans with my family, and I can't break them. I wish I could, though. Despite everything. I want to spend it with you."

"So you're choosing your family over me?"

"I don't see it that way, Klaus."

"Can I come with you?"

I hesitate. Open and close my mouth.

"What would I tell them?"

"I see." For a moment, I think he understands, and then I feel a familiar pinch at my neck. "I see you when you're sleeping, Snowflake. I know you're mine to take." Within seconds, the heavy drugs take me under.

CHAPTER 8
KLAUS

BIANCA LIES IN MY BED, wrapped in silk sheets, and suddenly, everything in the world is as it should be. She smells like vanilla and a peppermint twist, a mouth-watering combination that makes me want to lick every inch of her.

The drugs are still thick in her system, so she'll be out for a while. My Snowflake and I have fucked all the standard ways except anal, so I feel no guilt in stripping her naked and taking advantage of what I know to be mine, her tight body. I took off the majority of her clothes when I laid her down, but now I remove her bra and underwear, pressing the fabric to my nose as I peel her panties off. They're sopping. She's such a little slut for me.

I spread her limbs wide so I can look at every inch of her skin. She's completely splayed out, her dark curls fanned around her head, what feels like miles of perfect porcelain skin on display for me. I run a finger along the bottom of her foot just to watch her body twitch and jerk.

An electrifying sense of power comes with having her at my mercy, and I'm like a kid in Santa's Workshop, not sure which fascinating toy to play with first. Pushing her feet toward her ass and bending her knees, I dive right in and tongue her cunt.

At first, I'm just hungry for her taste, and then for the soft keening noise she makes as I lap her clit. I'm desperate to milk her for her cum, but I'd rather eat her cunt while she's awake to enjoy it and watch the shocked look in her eyes when she makes a mess all over me again.

I climb onto my knees between her spread legs, pull my cock out of my pants, and push her knees wide. Her skin is so incredibly pale, her raven black hair a shocking contrast. It's been that way since I first saw her, red-nosed and snowflakes sticking to her hair. While we've grown up apart, we're intrinsically connected, her in the spotlight and me in the shadows. Those two things haven't changed, and she practically glows for me.

When you grow up without a family, not really mattering to anyone, the kindness of a pretty girl means a lot.

I notch my cock up with her entrance. She's so tiny in every way except her tits and her ass, which are so full they make her look like she's begging to take dick. Still, I'm shocked her tight little pussy can stretch to accommodate me. I'm far from average. She whines as I press inside her, but no matter what I do, she won't wake up. The thought has me nearly blowing my load. What vile things could I do to her like this?

I spit on my finger and then reach around and play with her ass. I know I told myself I wouldn't fuck it, but I never said anything about this. I play with the tight little ring until it relaxes under the pressure. Eventually, I'm able to tuck the tip of my finger inside her as I feed my cock to her sleeping cunt. She parts her lips, gasping as her cunt kisses my balls.

Her ass isn't exposed enough for me, so I roll her onto her side, throw one long leg over my shoulder, and fuck her deep for a minute to make sure we're lined up right in this new position. She's moaning in her unconsciousness, and I tell myself she's begging for me to finger her ass. She loves it, and she wants more.

I spit on my finger again and very slowly work it into her ass. Little moans pour from the back of her throat, and all the muscles in her ass and cunt twitch as I fuck them both. So fucking tight. She was made for me to fuck, made to take my loads.

I rub my own dick through the thin separation of her ass and pussy, feeling like a God to be inside both holes, jerking myself off with her unconscious body, shoving my cock and fingers inside her and using her like a puppet. I need to stop gassing myself up like this, or I'm going to lose my load before I've had any real fun.

I pull out of her pussy with a hot, wet pop and climb up the bed until I'm straddling her chest. My thick cock hangs heavy, wiping her own pussy juice across her tits and over her nipples. I prop her head back, tip her chin up, and open her mouth. I admire her pretty pink tongue for a minute, stroke it with the tip of my index finger, then spit in her fucking mouth before shoving my cock straight down her throat.

She gags, and her throat flexes, trying to work me out. Her struggle is so fucking good, based on nothing but her unconscious need to survive. Weak kicks, twitching fingers. I hump her throat harder than I did her cunt, gagging her and listening to the sloppy sounds of her struggling to breathe. I'm a fucking goner this time, and I come down her throat so hard I see stars. My hips still as I lose my load, and I force myself to kick them forward a few more times, pumping every drop into her.

I pull out of her mouth with a pop. She's red this time but not turning purple, breathing fine, and I came so fucking hard. Leaning forward, I take her sleeping lips in mine, not caring that they taste like cum, just glad they're hers.

I can't quite get my dick hard again, but I'm not about to

squander an opportunity I've been waiting literal years for. I tuck myself back into my pants and search the room for some inspiration, something really fucking nasty I can do to her and tell her about in the morning. My gaze finds something just perfect for my sleeping Snowflake slut.

I gather the few necessary supplies, making sure the one item I'll be sticking inside her is meticulously clean. Then I put Snowflake facedown on a pillow and prop her ass in the air with her knees beneath her. Fuck, is she pretty all ready and spread out like this? I grab my phone and take a few pictures to remember the experience.

Cracking the seal on the bottle of lube I bought for Bianca a few months back, I start to gratuitously coat her pussy. I assumed I'd use it on her sooner, but my endgame has taken longer than I imagined. The brand-new candy cane decoration is round, thick, and just too damn big for Snowflake's tight little cunt. The thick swirl of red and white will look incredible inside her, and she won't remember if it hurts a little while I work it inside her.

I play with her clit for a few minutes, wishing I had come in her cunt instead. My cock twitches to life at the idea, and if I weren't already so invested in this plan, I would fuck her instead. Working my fingers into her one after the other, she's moaning, her eyes peeled ever so slightly back, but she's still not conscious. Her cunt trembles as I stretch her wider and wider. She comes around four of my fingers, keening softly as her cunt wrings me and juices drip down my wrist.

Well, that was fucking delicious and intensely helpful in sliding my thumb in. She's as loose as I'm going to get her without fisting her, and that's farther than I'm looking to stretch her tonight anyway. I pull out my hand and wipe her excess juices across her face. She's always so wet for me, and I want every inch of her to smell like this.

I line the end of the candy cane decoration up with her cunt and watch in wicked amusement as her puffy, swollen lips stretch to accommodate it. Her cheeks are as red as her cunt from all the intense sensation I'm forcing her body to accept with no outlet. I pour more lube over her cunt and watch it drip around the plastic struggling to fit inside her.

I lift her leg, angling her as I did while I was fucking her, and her pussy finally gives, accepting the oversized intrusion. We both come, her stretched farther than she's ever been in her life, clit red and swollen, practically pulsing from the pressure on her G-spot, and me coming in my pants at the sexiest sight I've ever seen—my girl stuffed and coming all over a candy cane.

With my cum still covering my cock, I lick her puffy lips around the plastic. I leave it exactly where it is since I worked really hard getting it in there. I snap one more picture for myself because really she's a magnificent sight, and then I climb into bed beside her to nap until she wakes up.

CHAPTER 9
BIANCA

MY EYES FLY OPEN, and I'm lying on the biggest bed in the largest room I've ever seen in my life. My heart races like I've run a marathon, and I look up through a canopy bed at vaulted ceilings. To my right is a row of floor-to-ceiling windows. Snow-covered hills peek out from behind heavy damask silk curtains.

The moon reflects off the snow, making things almost ghostly, and every inch of the room is black except for the red-and-gold accents. Strings of soft white light hang all around the space, giving it the appearance of a Christmas from a high-end designer magazine.

Where the hell am I?

And what the hell is shoved in my pussy?

It only takes me a moment to realize I'm stuffed fuller than I've ever been in my life, and I'm on the verge of what feels like not my first orgasm. Klaus's fingers move up and down my clit, and I look down to find a three-foot plastic candy cane sticking out of me. Thankfully, hook side out.

"What the fuck?" I shout before he latches his lips onto my clit and sucks until I'm not *near* an orgasm, but I'm screaming through it.

Once I finish shaking, moaning, and twitching, he gently removes the oversized intrusion and kisses all over my pussy.

"I had it in there an hour before you woke up. You're stretched wide open, baby. I can lick inside your whole cunt." He shoves his tongue in me to emphasize his point, and I moan at how raw, soothing, and hot it feels.

"I don't want my pussy stretched wide open. I want it tight," I complain, embarrassed that something that big fit inside me at all.

"You're *so* tight. It's not your fault. Cunts are made to stretch, and I'm a dirty pervert who wants to use you."

"Please, no more using. It hurts."

"I bet it does," he agrees but doesn't stop. "It's almost Christmas."

"I assumed it was already Christmas." Since he's not planning to stop, I prop myself up on my elbows to watch him as he kisses me. He's impossibly good looking; dark red, nearly black lashes fan his cheeks, and the softest sprinkle of freckles decorates his skin. His full lips are like sin as they kiss me.

"No, it's only ten. I didn't dose you as hard this time."

The casual way he refers to sticking a needle in my neck and drugging me is a little shocking, but it shouldn't be, coming from him.

"Thanks for the consideration." I sound exasperated, which is funny, given his mouth is all over me, but I realize he's honoring my request and not giving me more stimulation while still enjoying himself.

"This right here is the best present I've ever gotten."

He pulls my legs around his shoulders like a scarf.

"I doubt that."

"Well, I guess it's true I stole it rather than it being given to me, but my point still stands."

"You never got a bike or anything more fun to ride?"

He's quiet for a minute, lips pressing against me over and over. He works away from my pussy and on to my thighs, my lower belly. I'm giggling and soft, not fully caring that he made all these decisions for me once again.

"I've never been given a Christmas present officially, but I'm positive I'm enjoying this more than a bike."

The haze clears from my mind, and I comprehend his words more by the second. Those ones are especially hard to wrap my head around.

"What do you mean you've never been given a Christmas present?"

"Orphans aren't given presents, Snowflake."

"You're an orphan?" His words sink in, and while they hurt my heart, they also confuse me.

"Do I scream parental love to you?"

I think about that for a minute. "I guess not, but you're great with those kids."

He smiles at that, and it's soft and genuine. "Kids are good. They don't get fucked up until they're older, and if they're fucked up when they're little, you know the people responsible for loving them aren't doing enough of it. Most of the people who helped me when I was on my own were other kids, but no one like you. Adults were…" He shivers but doesn't continue.

How do I know him? When the hell have I ever known a little boy with red hair who never got a present? I know for a fact I wouldn't have ignored him. I would have helped him. I know all too well how it feels to be small and helpless.

While I'm worried about everything that's happened and what I'll tell my mom about my absence, I'm relieved he eliminated that problem. I don't want to see Richard this year and pretend I don't hate him, that he's not hurting my mom. Play nice, or she gets it worse. I just hope she doesn't have to suffer for me not showing at all.

I want to be with Klaus. I want to know how we met and why he's so obsessed with me. What did I ever do to deserve this attention that makes me feel electric, alive, and possibly like the most evil and selfish person in existence?

"How do we know each other, Klaus?"

I grab his hair and pull, like he's done to me so many times, and force him away from my achingly sore lips. To my surprise, he relents, climbing over my body, dragging his warm skin along mine, his chest bare, his pants still on. He kisses my lips, letting me taste myself, and then lies beside me.

"I was hoping you would remember on your own. It's no fun for anyone if you tell."

"I don't remember, Klaus. Please." I've been racking my brain since he let it slip, and I've come up with nothing. A lot of spots in my memory aren't super clear, but I can't imagine how I don't remember him.

"My parents were extremely wealthy before they died, but I don't remember any of that. I grew up with my mother's grandmother, but she couldn't touch the money. I'm not even sure if she knew there was anything left to get. We were poor. I was a burden. She hated me."

"She died when I was five, not that I remember much from living with her, and then I moved from place to place. First with foster families, and eventually, I ran away when I was eleven. I didn't realize I had an inheritance waiting for me. I didn't realize there were options. I was alone. I was hungry, and I was picking pockets at a Christmas fair on a tree farm."

His words unlock a memory from a time so dark most things are missing. My mother married Richard the previous year, and he was beating the hell out of us regularly. He took us to the Christmas fair to keep up appearances, but we were both sporting bruised ribs, and Mom had a ring of bruises around her neck that looked much worse than my own.

I was freezing cold, thirteen, and I remember thinking I'd rather be dead than go home to that big house, bigger than we'd ever had before, and watch this man beat her. I rode the carousel twice because Richard thought I should even though I felt too old, too broken for things like that.

I didn't even care so much what he did to me, but if I didn't listen, my mother got it too.

"*Smile,*" he shouted as he took pictures to show to people who would praise him for taking on another man's kid, being the father I needed.

I hop off the horse and walk back over to them, awaiting my next instructions. He leads us to another section of the fair with my mother and me both in step behind him. A bright flash of red hair interrupts all the white and green as a boy about my age runs between us, knocking me to the ground and distracting Richard long enough to fish the wallet out of his pocket.

Richard is confused for only a moment before he spots the boy, wallet still in his hand. The kid runs, and Richard chases him. He's thin and quick, but not enough, and the muscled, full-grown man grabs him by his shoulder and throws him to the ground. He's about to kick the boy, not even worried about how easy it would be to pluck the wallet out of his grasp. My mother doesn't even look surprised, just lost.

The boy is too skinny for his age, too small and dirty. Something is seriously wrong, and a protective instinct swells up inside me as I jump between them, and Richard kicks me instead. His boot collides with my already bruised ribs, and I lie on top of the boy as I brokenly cry. It's quiet, and we're far enough away from the crowd that no one hears. My mother runs over, grabbing his arm and begging him not to make a scene. People will see.

For a moment, Richard leaves me lying on top of him, struggling to catch my breath, and the boy whispers in my ear.

"Everything is okay. You kept me safe, and now I'll do the same for you. I'm going to make sure you're okay."

Richard rips me off him and to my feet, dragging me straight back to the car. The boy gets up and runs into the treeline, and the last thing I remember thinking was that I preferred it being me. Richard beat me again when we got home, but that night was the last time he hit me.

I roll over and face Klaus, really seeing him for the first time.

"I remember."

And he kisses me. It's long and sweet, full of feelings I didn't know he was capable of. There's no rough agony, no pain, just the adoring lips of someone who has spent most of his life obsessed with me, adoring me at long last.

"You're the only person to ever take a hit for me, Snowflake, and I have never stopped watching you."

"Where have you been all this time?"

"With you, Snowflake, always with you."

"How?"

"That money my parents left for me? It was a lot. I got it when I turned eighteen, and that's when I went from your adoring fan sleeping in the streets and hanging out in the shadows just to be near you to a man who could take care of you and provide for you."

I absorb that, and his startling green eyes stick to my face. "You slept outside my window?"

"Yes. Anywhere I could be near you."

"Speaking of providing for me, have you really been paying my rent?" A sliver of discomfort snakes through me.

"Yes, you have a savings account with seventy-five thousand dollars for when you graduate. You won't have a speck of debt, and you'll have paid for it yourself." He says the words pointedly like he knows how much it means to me to do things by myself, but it's a con, and we both know it.

"I paid for it myself while *you* paid for my rent."

"Semantics," he answers with a wink, obviously knowing how hard it is for me to accept this kind of thing when I associate an upgrade in living situations with being beaten daily. He knows all too well what happened in that house.

"Why did he stop after that?"

"I put a gun in his face and told him I'd blow his brains out if he touched you again. I guess he realized I wasn't bluffing."

"Why didn't you just kill him?" I sound disappointed, whining even, and I know it's not what a good person would ask, but I wish he had.

"Because I was thirteen, Snowflake. I wasn't a killer yet. I became one for you."

My heart stops, and my breath catches.

"What does that mean?"

"He's the last living person who's ever hurt you in any real way. You've never noticed your bullies disappear? The people who want to hurt you all seem to just fall away? The people who robbed you of your good nature, or didn't pay their portion of the bills, or ate the food meant for you all never came back."

He killed my ex-roommates. Probably Lydia Herringer, who loved to mercilessly tease me and went missing in tenth grade.

"I… I never really thought about it."

"You didn't have to because I've always taken care of them for you. I always will."

"How many people, Klaus?" My voice shakes, my stomach turning in unease.

"A lot, Snowflake."

I let that sink in. I have two choices, I believe, to decide whether or not this is a situation I can be happy with. How much do I really care about what he is versus what he's done for me? I knew he killed Ralph. I watched him murder that pervert from the mall. He may have kidnapped me, but I'm surely not fighting to get away from him right now.

What are a few more deaths when he's never given me a

choice anyway? I'm not going to escape him. I never have. So my options are happiness or misery, and I think I might be in love with this fucked-up man who no one has ever loved, who has only ever loved me.

"Wait a minute. My ex-boyfriends are still alive. If you've been following me since I was thirteen, you've seen…"

My cheeks turn bright red.

"You fuck other guys while I waited for you? You have two ex-boyfriends who are currently living out of the four, and they treated you well. You were happy, and I couldn't be there for you yet. Plus, I told you I'm a pervert. I didn't mind watching until I was ready to make my move. By the time you moved in with Gina, I was done sharing."

"Have you…?" I'm unable to ask the question when it doesn't seem fair since he literally watched me fuck other people, but I care.

"How the hell could I do that when you're the only girl in the world?" He shakes his head like I'm crazy. "I do get a sexual thrill from killing, though, if I'm perfectly honest."

"You were a virgin?" I nearly shout, more concerned about his lack of sexual experience than I am with the fact that mayhem and bloodshed make his dick hard. I guess I'm not entirely surprised, considering how he fucked me after his two most recent murders.

"I've been paying attention to how you come for a long time, Snowflake." He's wearing an arrogant smile.

My mind is reeling. My body is warm from him pressed against every inch of me, and despite everything he's said, I don't even consider pulling away. He's evil. He's twisted. He's my everything. I was his first.

"Is your name really Klaus?"

"It was at one point. It's the name I used when we met."

"I like it." I run my fingers through his thick red hair. It's so damn soft.

"Then I'll keep this one."

"What about this place? Is it yours?"

"One of many, but it's not owned by Klaus." He laughs, and that sound tells me he's full of mischief.

"Should I ask?"

"No, Snowflake, I think it's best to let me keep my secrets."

CHAPTER 10
BIANCA

I WAKE on Christmas morning to the delicious scent of bacon. The twinkling lights of Klaus's room add the softest, loveliest ambiance, and I reach out to touch him, still feeling soft and cuddly after the night before. My hand finds nothing but cold sheets.

Climbing out of bed, I stretch my incredibly overused body and groan as all the knots and kinks make themselves known. I throw on the fluffy robe he's left out for me and smile at how absurdly thoughtful this naughty, murderous man is. Merry Christmas to me.

I step out of his room, not really knowing where I'm going since I've never been anywhere in his house but the bedroom and the en suite bath when I peed in the middle of the night. I'm immediately shocked to find the rest of the place doesn't have the same black decor.

The hall is white and not all that long. There's a blue accent wall. I come around the corner and find a wall made of logs and windows revealing the wintery mountainside. Holy shit, we're in a cabin.

I walk through a living room decorated like a designer catalog. It's snowing and perfectly Christmas. The tree is at least twelve feet tall, and I've never seen so many presents in my life. He really was planning and preparing for this.

The place is gorgeous but not as large as I imagined. The enormous bedroom probably takes half the space. I follow the scent of bacon down the hall and a small set of steps into the kitchen. I smile at Klaus's muscular back in front of the stove, cooking the bacon I smelled.

I know my mom will be pissed as hell I'm not spending Christmas with her, and Richard will be mad he doesn't have a picture for social media to prove what a wonderful and doting father and husband he is, but I'm thrilled. After learning what I have about Klaus and his history with my stepfather, I'm especially happy to avoid him.

This Christmas morning is everything I've ever wanted.

"Morning, Santa," I say cheerily as I pop into the room, still sexed up and feeling sweet after learning the extent of his devotion to me. I slide my hands over his sides, wrapping my arms around him.

"Hey, Snowflake." He turns around quickly, kisses me, then tries to usher me out of the room. "Why don't you go sit by the tree and check out which presents are yours? Hint: it's all of them. I'll grab you when breakfast is done, and then we can open them."

He kisses me again and squeezes my ass. It's so normal and domestic that my brain short-circuits, and I think I've actually gone insane. He's watching me process all this with his usual smile, like he's never hacked a man apart with an axe in his life.

"Come on." He waves me toward the door, nudging lightly when I don't budge. "Snowflake, stop being suspicious. There's absolutely nothing—"

The sounds of bound and struggling people coming from the other room interrupt his bullshit. My head snaps in that direction, and Klaus pushes me back harder.

"Klaus, what the fuck? Who is that?"

"Now, now, Snowflake. We were having such a nice evening and morning. At least get settled before you ask questions. Do you want coffee? It's gingerbread flavored like you like, and I have some revolting eggnog-flavored creamer."

That actually does sound excellent, but I'm pretty sure the other Christmas kidnap victims are more important than my holiday sweet tooth.

"I don't fucking think so, Klaus. Who is in there?"

He sighs like I'm the one being ridiculous, and I push past him. There's a dining room adjoining the kitchen with a long table set with tapered candles, fancy plates, and my mother and stepfather bound and gagged seated on opposite sides of the table.

Mom's makeup is already done, so he must have grabbed them this morning, but her tears have destroyed her mascara. Her lipstick is smudged around the gag in her mouth, and while she looks disheveled, I don't think he's hurt her. Richard, on the other hand, is beat to shit.

His gray hair appears to be missing tufts, and he has two black eyes. I imagine there are more injuries. He's a big man and wouldn't go down easily. I look at Klaus, realizing he has a bruise on his cheek for the first time.

I stop dead in my tracks, my heart pounding as I start to get an idea of what Klaus intends to do. I don't give a fuck about Richard. Klaus could have killed him years ago, and I would have appreciated it, but my mother is another story. She's weak, not evil.

"Not my mom, Klaus." My voice is so pathetically small, but he can't hurt her. I'll do anything to keep him from hurting her.

He tilts his head to the side, looking me up and down.

"Snowflake, you're coming very close to insulting me again. Do you really think I plan to hurt your mother?"

"I don't know." I decide that an honest answer is better than a lie, even if I do insult him.

He reaches out an oversized hand and gently strokes my cheek. "Your mother is only bound because she refused to be agreeable. I have not and have no intentions to hurt her."

I let out a deep breath. That was all I needed to know.

"However, I must point out that she's rather bruised, and that's not my doing." He points the bacon grease-covered fork he was cooking with at Richard, who is watching us with genuine murderous hatred. I watch him over Klaus's shoulder, insidious fear snaking through me. "I should have put your mother on the no-touching list a long time ago. I apologize for that."

"Uh-huh." I can practically hear the threats my stepfather aims at me.

"Snowflake, are you ignoring me?" he asks. And I guess I am because I missed the last thing he said.

He follows my gaze to Richard tied to that chair, promising me with his eyes that he will do the most awful things he possibly can the moment he gets loose. I also don't see any confusion.

Where Mom is terrified and confused, my stepfather knows why they're here. He recognizes the red-headed boy who put a gun in his face and told him to stop beating his stepdaughter or die.

"Why are you looking at her like that, Rich?" Klaus cocks his head to the side. "Are you wishing you could do something to her? Maybe kick her in the ribs again? Your wife over there not enough for you to beat on? You think you can touch what's mine?"

Richard's gagged so he can't answer, but every muscle in his body strains and twitches against his bindings like he's trying to get free and do just that. He wants to kill every one of us. He doesn't even seem afraid for Mom, the woman he claims he loves so much in their staged social media posts.

"Snowflake, are you actually afraid right now? I think I may be angry that you don't trust me to keep you safe."

"Yes, I'm afraid." And I really am. "I told you how I felt." I wanted him gone. I wish you killed him. He's the thing I have nightmares about.

"Well, this isn't half as fun as I hoped it would be. I don't want you to be afraid. I wanted to give you a sense of righteous victory. It's Christmas, for God's sake!"

"Are you actually pouting right now, Klaus?"

He comes over to me, touches my cheeks, and looks into my eyes. "I wanted your Christmas to be perfect, and you wanted to spend it with your family." That mischievous smile tells me he's just being a prick about what I said in that hallway on Christmas Eve.

"Are you seriously doing this, Klaus?"

"Wait, wait, one minute. I can fix this. New plan!"

He heads back to the kitchen with what is most definitely not a new plan.

It's just me, Mom, and Richard. I'm shaking as he grunts and does his best to break his way free. Mom begs me with her eyes to do something, but I can't. I just stand there until Klaus returns.

He walks back into the room, and I don't even see the knife in his hand until he plunges it into Richard's stomach. He shoves it into him as hard and fast as he plunged his cock into me that first night, his first time. I'm as sick as him because I'm turned on by the thought and the violence. I loathe my stepfather.

Klaus leaves the knife in his gut and takes a step back, admiring his work. Mom screams until the sound suddenly cuts off, and I think she passed out. Richard stares at Klaus instead of me, and that murderous intention fades with the severity of the gut wound.

I assume Klaus will pull the knife out and stab him again and again, like he did with the axe and that man at the

Christmas tree farm. Instead, he stands beside me, and we both watch as the man who tormented me and my mother slowly, painfully bleeds to death. His gag stays in his mouth, and Klaus offers him no last words.

He's dead when my mom comes to.

She's confused for a split second before she realizes her husband is gone and starts screaming again. Klaus shakes his head like his plan isn't working out, but I know better. He's enjoying the hell out of himself.

I'm shaking. I must be in shock as I watch the situation above my body rather than in it. So fucked in the head from all the death, I can't stay in my own brain.

"Sit down before you pass out, Bianca. I don't want to wind up sitting in the hospital on Christmas."

I pull out a chair and sit. I place my feet on the carpet as Richard's blood begins to snake past on the hardwood floor.

Klaus heads back to the kitchen, opening and closing cabinets, stomping, loudly letting us know exactly how much time we have before his return. My mother stares into my eyes, begging me to release her, but I don't. I lay my head on the table. Richard is dead beside us, and I'm definitely in shock, but I still trust Klaus not to hurt her. He didn't hurt those kids.

He comes back into the room and places a plate in front of each of us except for Richard, and part of me thought he might just to be funny. As he puts the plate in front of my mother, he stands behind her, and her tears pick up in intensity.

"Come on, Mom. Stop crying! I know this wasn't the best first introduction, but we're going to be family, so we need to get used to one another." He pulls the gag out of her mouth. Tears stream down her face, and she's staring at me like I can give her some form of explanation.

"Oh my God. Oh dear God. Bianca, what is happening? Richard, no, please no."

Klaus unbinds her hands so she can eat but leaves her legs and body tied to the chair. He takes his own seat beside me and pulls his bacon and eggs over to him, quickly digging in like he's starving.

Of course neither of us touches our food. He finally looks toward my mother with a forced politeness I've never seen, an apology in his expression.

"It's a family rule that we don't spend Christmas with women beaters, Sharon. Your daughter is my family now." Klaus grabs my hand in his like we're presenting a united front.

"You literally murdered someone on Christmas," I snap. Staring at Richard's corpse, then my bound and crying mother, and finally the crazy fuck I've chosen not to try to escape from.

"I still don't beat women." His face pinches like I've really pissed him off this time. "Now eat your fucking eggs. You have a lot of presents to open." He turns to my sobbing mother with a broad smile. "Don't worry, Mom, I picked some nice things out for you too. Your favorite color is still teal, right?"

No one answers him.

"I'm trying to make a good impression on your mother, Snowflake. You could try to be helpful." He shrugs toward her like she and I are the unreasonable ones despite the kidnapping and the corpse.

"You stabbed her husband in the gut and let him bleed out slowly. Minutes ago, Klaus."

Mom wails, her tears choking her. "Please, God, please!"

"Oh, fine!" Klaus slaps the table, and the sudden violence shocks her into quieting down. "No more begging. Who can wait? Presents now."

I still haven't taken a single bite of my food. I haven't checked, but common sense tells me Richard is still warm, and if I look closely enough, little rivulets of blood continue to drain out of him. I possibly could have saved him. I chose not to.

Klaus lifts the entire chair my mother is tied to and carries her out of the room.

"Come on, Snowflake. The tree is in here."

I follow him back to the living room and the beautiful view of the mountains. He places my mother in front of the fire, and she doesn't even try to fight him despite her arms being free.

"Mom, you're not going to die," I try to reassure her.

"Merry Christmas!" Klaus says as he shoves a present in my face.

"Merry Christmas, Klaus."

EPILOGUE
KLAUS

I WALK DOWN the hall of Sunrise Mental Health Services, hands in my pockets, whistling a holiday tune even though it's officially the new year. I reach my psychiatrist's door and knock in the pattern of the song I'm singing.

"Come in."

I open the door, observing without surprise his office is exactly the same as it was before the season. What would be so bad about a little holiday cheer? I myself have buckets of it.

"Hey, Dr. Shane, how are you doing today?" I ask as I hop over the back of his couch and land on the cushions just to irritate him. I like my shrink, but he's uptight. He pulls his notepad out of his desk, pen in hand.

"James," he greets me with another fake name. People all over the world call me different things. "How are you doing this week? Anything new you'd like to discuss? It's been a while since our last session, and I admit I was nervous about you." He's already making notes, and I haven't said anything but how are you.

I smile, knowing that he won't like my big news. "Well, I finally made my move with that girl."

He pauses in his note-taking, looking up at me as he

understands what I'm saying. I've told him all about the fantasies I've had of abducting my little Snowflake and fucking her in all sorts of nasty ways while she begs and cries but never gives me permission. I've told him about some of the people I've killed too, and I don't think my doctor is such a good person, seeing as he hasn't reported me.

"You didn't do something that can't be undone, did you?" He knows damn well those are my favorite things to do. He's the one who has helped guide and mold me into something close to productive, something able to survive in this world.

"I've done a lot of things that can't be undone. You know if you drop a plate, it doesn't mend simply because it was an accident." I smirk at him as he tilts his head to the side.

"While I'm glad you've been listening, the extensiveness and complexity of your notes and surveillance wouldn't convince a single judge or jury that anything you've done to her is an accident."

"You're much too serious, Dr. Shane. She fell in love with me, just like I told you she would. I didn't need to snap her neck or anything."

"You just wanted to."

"I always want to hurt her, but if I play too rough, I don't get to play again. You know the most important part of all of this is keeping her safe."

"Do you love her, James?"

"She's the best present I've ever gotten."

ALSO BY AURELIA KNIGHT

In the mood for another dark holiday novella?

Knives and Kisses

Coming February 1st 2024

Want to meet Doctor Shane and see where the series began?

Read Mind to Bend

For a golden retriever serial killer who would do anything for his "Little Nun" Read Vow to Sever

Mafia boss intent on killing her whole family and everything she loves? Preorder Dynasty to Destroy

For a medium dark, nerdy heroine, secret crime family trilogy, check out The Illicit Library Collection books 1-3

Complete and free to read in Kindle Unlimited!

ABOUT AURELIA

Aurelia Knight is a hot mess, doing her best to keep it together most days. Words are the greatest love of her life second only to her husband and sons. If she's not typing away, getting lost in her own world, she's reading and slipping away into the worlds of other writers. A caffeine addict who believes sleep is secondary to the endless promise of "just one more chapter".

For the most up to date information join Aurelia's reader group on Facebook, Aurelia's Illicit Library, and subscribe to her mailing list at www.AureliaKnight.com

ACKNOWLEDGMENTS

A special thanks to my beta team! I hope your stockings are full of goodies instead of coal, you naughty bitches.

And to the wonderful professionals who helped make this project possible:

Editing by Jenny Simms with Editing4Indies

Proofing by Amy Perkins with Nerdy Girl Collective

Character Art by Cuckooboo

Cover Design by Kirsty Still of Pretty Little Design Co

Made in the USA
Middletown, DE
08 December 2024